D1527361

A SPELL TO TELL

A LEMON TEA COZY MYSTERY

LUCY MAY

This is a work of fiction. Names, characters, businesses, places, events and incidents are either the products of the author's imagination or used in a fictitious manner. Any resemblance to actual persons, living or dead, or actual events is purely coincidental.

Copyright © 2018 Lucy May

All rights reserved.

ISBN: 1987456521

ISBN 13: 978-1987456523

Cover design by Cosmic Letterz

No part of this book may be reproduced in any form or by any electronic or mechanical means, including information storage and retrieval systems, without written permission from the author, except for the use of brief quotations in a book review.

❀ Created with Vellum

DEDICATION

To those who believe in magic.

Sign up for my newsletter for information on new releases!
https://lucymayauthor.com/subscribe

Follow me!
https://www.facebook.com/lucymayauthor/
lucy@lucymayauthor.com

CHAPTER 1

"*A*re you ready for this?" I asked Daphne, taking several calming breaths.

She smiled. "Girl, I've been ready for the last three months. I didn't think this moment would ever come. I don't think I realized how much work would be involved just to get the place transformed into a bakery. I thought it would be a few ovens and sinks and then some seating in the dining room. This has been gobs of work."

Smiling, I looked around the tiny dining area of our new bakery. Today was our grand opening. I was nervous and excited at the same time.

"You've got the cash drawer in?" I asked, going through a mental checklist.

"Yes."

"Tables are cleaned, condiment bar stocked, display ready," I mumbled, as I spun around. Everything had to be just perfect.

"We're good, Violet. This is going to be great. There's already buzz around town after our soft opening last week. This is going to do fabulous! Are you ready?"

On the heels of another breath, I closed my eyes and composed myself. "Okay, I'm ready. Hit it."

She flipped the switch on the neon 'open' sign, and we were officially open for business. We both stood in the center of the dining room, staring at the front door. Daphne burst out giggling.

"I don't think there's going to be a stampede."

I laughed with her. "No, probably not. That was a little anti climatic."

Another giggle from her as she walked behind the counter, taking her position at the register. "Was it like this at your other bakery?"

I shook my head. "Not really, but I was opening in a larger city on a busy street. There had been a lot of buzz before we opened. The first few days we were slammed and then things tapered off. Fortunately, after a month or so, business picked back up and steadily increased. It took people a while for word to travel. So many cafes and other stores had been in that same space, no one took us seriously at first."

"Tara is going to do great. She seemed pretty excited to take over full-time," she said, referring to my manager for the bakery I'd left behind when I moved.

"Yeah, she'll be fabulous. She's been my assistant for over two years. She's more than ready to run the whole show. I couldn't close it. That store was my baby. I nurtured it for so long, I couldn't let it go."

Daphne flashed a grin. "Now, you're officially a chain!"

I laughed. "I don't know if two bakeries make a chain, but you're a part of that chain as well if they do."

"Divine Desserts will soon be in every city!" Daphne teased.

"Yeah, let's not get ahead of ourselves," I warned.

We both stood behind the counter, waiting for our first customer. I knew the risks of opening a business in a small town, but Daphne was confident we could do it. It wouldn't be a booming business, but I was certain we could make it profitable. I was actually looking forward to the slower pace a small town bakery would offer. I was completely at peace with working eight-hour days instead of twelve or more.

When the first customer walked through the door, we both froze. "Hi," I finally greeted the elderly man who was scrutinizing the cookies in the case.

"Can I offer you a sample?" Daphne volunteered.

The man studied the assortment of cookies and finally settled on a baker's dozen of chocolate chip cookies. Daphne rang him up while I restocked.

"That was kind of intense," I whispered to Daphne once the man was gone. "He didn't look happy, like we forced him to come in and buy cookies."

"That's just Grumpy Gus. Don't you remember him?" she asked.

My eyes widened, "He's still alive?"

That made her giggle. "Yes, he's still alive. He's the town grump and clearly not ready to give up his role anytime soon."

I nodded in understanding. Gus had been old when I was little. That made him close to a relic now. It had been so long since I'd seen him, I hadn't recognized him.

The little bells above the door jingled again. We looked up to see my mother coming through the door. She glanced around the empty bakery before her gaze made its way to us, tension lining her features.

"Slow start?"

"It'll pick up. We've only been open five minutes, after all. People may not even realize we're here yet," I explained, hoping to calm my own nerves as well as Daphne's.

"Well, it's good no one's here. I need to talk to you. Both of you," she said, flicking her eyes between us.

3

"What's up?" I asked, assuming it was something to do with the coven.

"There's been a theft," she announced.

Daphne and I looked at each other and then back at my mother. "A theft?"

She nodded her head, looked back at the door and then leaned over the counter. "At the museum."

"Lemon Bliss has a museum?" I asked in bewilderment.

My mother rolled her eyes. "Oh good grief, Violet! Do you remember anything from growing up here?"

I looked to Daphne for help. "You know, the old museum. It's really an old house. There isn't too much in there, just stuff that showcases the history of Lemon Bliss," she explained.

"Oh," I said. With her prompt, I recalled visiting the place when we had been in grade school. It was small and only open a day or two a week. It wasn't exactly a main tourist attraction.

"What was stolen?" Daphne asked.

My mother ran one of her hands over her black hair, her bracelets clinking as she smoothed back the stray strands that had fallen loose from the knot atop her head.

"Several items, but two are of serious concern for us. There will be a coven meeting tomorrow night to discuss the issue," she said in a low voice.

"Mom, there's no one here," I reminded her.

"I know that," she shot back, her irritation evident.

Daphne reached out and squeezed my mother's hand. "We'll be there. I'm sure it will be fine. There's nothing to worry about."

"If only that were true," she muttered as she stepped back from the counter.

"Do you want a doughnut or a muffin?" I asked, hoping to nudge her mind off of her worries. I never quite knew how seriously to take my mother. She tended toward dramatic. Only occasionally were her theatric reactions justified.

"No thank you. I need to talk to Lila. I'll see you girls tomorrow, and good luck with your grand opening. I'll be sure to pass along the word that you're open and ready for business," she said, waving as she walked out. The sound of charm bracelets jingling followed her out the door.

"That was weird," Daphne said, once the door fell closed behind my mother. "Virginia is not one to get worked up about anything."

I shrugged a shoulder. "She's still on edge about the death of that supernatural investigator in the factory. She's been waiting for the other shoe to drop for months. I keep telling her we're fine and there's nothing to worry about, but she is convinced she senses something coming."

"Well, I think your mom might be someone I would trust in that department," Daphne said, her brow furrowing. "I just hope it isn't another murder."

We were interrupted when another customer came through the door, followed by a steady stream of people for the next couple of hours. The sales depleted many of the cookies and muffins, which meant it was time to start baking. I loved baking and was more than happy to leave the front of the bakery to Daphne while I put on my apron and got to work.

"Hey," she popped her head in the kitchen a while later.

"Hi. How's it going out there?"

She shook her head. "Ever get what you asked for and then regret it?"

I chuckled as I carefully filled muffin cups with batter. "Yep. Pretty busy out there?"

"We're almost completely wiped out of cookies. I just sold our last blueberry muffin as well."

I nodded and pointed to a cooling rack filled with blueberry muffins. "Those are ready to go. There are peanut butter cookies in the oven, and I'll get started on chocolate chip as soon as I get these in the oven," I replied, entirely in my element.

Daphne nodded and carried the muffins out to the front. I could hear the bells jingle and knew another customer was coming in. That was definitely a good sign.

I spent the next several hours baking muffins and cookies, and fielding questions about the specialty cakes we were offering. Daphne managed to secure several orders, mostly for birthdays, and one anniversary cake. I could feel the strain of the day's business getting to me and couldn't wait to get home and put up my feet.

"Can I kiss the cook?" a deep voice cut through my thoughts just as I was slicing through a piecrust.

I smiled and turned to face Gabriel Trahan. "There you are."

"I stopped by earlier, but poor Daphne looked like she was overwhelmed. I figured I'd come back when things had slowed down," he said, leaning in and giving me a quick kiss.

"It's been busy."

"Here, I thought you could use this," he said, handing me a cup of coffee from Crooked Coffee, my favorite local coffee shop in Lemon Bliss.

"Thank you. Daphne is still planning on moving forward with her coffee shop plan," I laughed. "She may change her mind after today."

"She looks like she might be getting tired. Are you guys going to hire any help?"

"That's the plan, but we wanted to see what we needed. This first month, it will just be the two of us. My mom and her friends have offered to help if we need it. Considering how busy we are on a Tuesday, I think we may need them for this Saturday," I said, sliding a tray of cookies into the oven.

"I'm here for you as well. I may not be as pretty as the ladies, but I can sell a doughnut or two," he said with that familiar grin that never failed to send a curl of warmth through me.

"We might take you up on that, which means you might live to regret it," I countered with a wink.

He chuckled. "I'll let you get back to work. I just wanted to stop by and tell you good luck, but I don't think you need it. I'll call you tonight and you can fill me in on the rest of the day," he said, giving me another quick kiss before slipping out the back door.

I sipped my coffee, savoring the rich flavor and the kick of caffeine. I could've used a second wind, and this might do the trick. I still had tons of baking to prep for tomorrow. We were definitely going to need to hire an assistant. I could keep up for now, but I certainly didn't want to work at this pace forever.

"I'm so tired. I'm going straight home, crawling into a hot bubble bath and drinking a glass of wine," Daphne said as she came through the kitchen door.

"Are we closed?" I asked in surprise.

She nodded. "It's four. We're officially done for the day."

"Oh, now it's time to clean up," I said with a wink.

"Oh no, you're kidding right?"

I shook my head. "We can't leave it looking like this. It won't take long. You take care of the front, and I'll finish up back here."

She was mumbling as she headed out. "Who thought this was a good idea?"

"You did!" I shouted.

Despite the physical exhaustion, I was charged with energy. The day had been hectic, but I thrived on the adrenaline rush. I knew it wouldn't always be like this. I wanted to cherish the moment, even if I was so tired I could barely stand.

I'd reluctantly returned to Lemon Bliss, Louisiana for what I thought would be a temporary visit several months ago. In short order, I'd learned I was a witch descended from generations of witches, gotten caught up in the investigation of a suspicious murder at the defunct lemon tea factory I'd inherited from my grandmother, and reconnected with a few old friends. I'd come back to my hometown with no intention of staying, only to discover I didn't want to leave.

Hey, I had witchy things to learn. Plus, my old bestie, Daphne, persuaded me that Lemon Bliss was in need of a bakery and we were the ones to make it happen. It was a win for our 'official' opening day to be a success.

I took one last look around the kitchen and declared it was clean and ready to go tomorrow morning. I was going to come in early and get a head start on the baking.

"Ready?" I asked Daphne who was stocking napkins at the counter.

"Yes! Let's get out of here."

We walked out together, locked up and went our separate ways. We were both too tired for chitchat. As I walked to my car, I thought about my mother's visit and how upset she had been. I hoped it wasn't anything serious. I didn't have the time to worry about another threat to the witches in Lemon Bliss.

CHAPTER 2

*I*t was too early. Mere months ago, rising with the sun at the crack of dawn was such a habit, I managed it even when I was tired. Since I'd moved to Lemon Bliss a few months ago, I'd gotten out of practice. Seriously out of practice. This morning, I had to force myself out of bed. Now that Daphne and I had opened the bakery, I needed to get back in the swing of things and fast.

My eyes were still a little blurry as I stumbled out of the house and headed for my car. I was meeting Gabriel at Crooked Coffee before I headed for the bakery. We didn't open for customers until eight. That gave me plenty of time to get a few things started before any customers arrived.

Despite my half-awake haze, just the thought of baking made me smile. I loved to bake. Even though I'd had my doubts about it, now that we had opened the bakery, I was thrilled. My world had been turned inside out a few months back when I came to Lemon Bliss for what was supposed to be nothing more than a visit. Ha! My visit had turned into much more.

I might've been tired, but I was glad Lemon Bliss was

home once again and even more so that I was back to baking. Rolling my car to a stop in front of Crooked Coffee, I glanced up at the massive oak tree that had been split down the center and grown crookedly as a result. Shaking my head, I chuckled to myself as I turned to go into the coffee shop. All those years, I'd thought lightning split the tree. I couldn't have guessed it was a witch's spell gone awry, but then I also couldn't have guessed I was a witch back then either.

"Good morning," Gabriel said with a smile as I slipped into the chair across from him. "I already ordered for you."

With an appreciative smile, I curled my hand around the warm cup of coffee and took a sip. I loved caffeine, seriously loved it. "Thank you," I said with a sigh as I set the cup down. "I don't think I could have handled waiting even a minute longer."

"Did you get some sleep last night?"

"I did. I have a feeling today is going to be busier. I hate to drink and run, but I need to get over to the bakery in the next half hour or so," I explained, feeling a little guilty for rushing out the door.

"When are you going to hire some help? Both of you looked worn out yesterday."

I laughed. "Is that a nice way of saying I looked awful? You really need to work on your game. That's no way to woo a woman."

Gabriel's mouth hitched at the corner as he winked. "I don't need to woo you. I have you."

I felt my cheeks heat, but I rolled my eyes. Gabriel was too charming for his own good. "Maybe so, but at least pretend I didn't look terrible yesterday."

His grin widened. "Of course not. You just looked busy and tired. That's it. I take it as a good sign. Day one and y'all were busy."

I couldn't help my own proud smile. "We'll see how the

first thirty days go and then we'll talk about hiring some help. We can't spend money we don't have. It could all dry up today or tomorrow," I said.

"I love it when you talk business."

That deserved a full eye roll. "Okay, thanks for the coffee, but I've only got a few more minutes."

"No worries. How's your mom? I saw her yesterday and she looked like she was worked up about something. Is everything okay?"

I sighed. "I don't know. She was in a tizzy. I guess someone broke into the museum and stole some stuff. I don't know why she's so freaked out about it, but I'm supposed to meet her tonight."

He slowly nodded his head. "I heard about the break in, but I didn't think it was a big deal."

"I don't see how it can be, but she certainly thinks it is. Needless to say, Daphne and I have been summoned to another meeting tonight."

"Oh, one of those secret witch meetings I'm not supposed to know about?" he asked with a grin.

"Shh, they'll kill me if they know you know. I could get ousted or flogged or have some crazy spell cast on me. I don't know what witches do to other witches."

He shrugged a shoulder. "I think they all know I know, but like to pretend otherwise. Don't forget Aunt Coral is one of the old guard witches," he said, referring to his aunt.

I laughed at the absurdity of our conversation. It was rather ridiculous to be having coffee and chatting about witches.

"I forgot we even had a museum in Lemon Bliss. Have you ever been?" I asked him.

"Nope. I guess it never really interested me."

I chuckled and nodded my head. "I haven't been there since elementary school. If I remember right, there are some antiques and papers and whatnot from the settling of

11

Lemon Bliss. I know my family donated some stuff. Maybe my mom's upset because a family heirloom was taken," I reasoned.

He didn't look convinced. "I don't know. Aunt Coral seemed pretty rattled by it as well."

I didn't get a chance to say any more.

"How was opening day?" Sheriff Harold Smith said, materializing beside our table.

Glancing up, I found him peering down at me. The man had an intense way of looking at me. I tended to feel as if something was out of place whenever he did. I self-consciously ran a hand over my hair.

"It was great," I replied, taking a sip of coffee to mask my nervousness.

The dust had only recently settled from the accidental death in the lemon tea factory. During the sheriff's investigation of that, he'd kept me under the microscope the entire time, certain I knew something about my mother and her friends that he didn't. Of course, he was right. It just wasn't anything about the death in the factory. It was the fact they were all witches, the lot of them, myself included. With a mental shake, I kept my attention on him.

"Suppose you heard about the trouble over at the museum?" he asked, his tone stern.

Exchanging a glance with Gabriel, I looked up to find Harold's eyes boring into me once again.

Clearing my throat, I found my voice. "My mother mentioned it yesterday."

"Know anything about it?" he asked.

"No, I don't. I've been pretty busy the past several weeks trying to get a business off the ground," I said tersely.

Gabriel gave me a warning look that told me to cool my jets.

"If you hear anything, I'd appreciate you letting me

know. You might overhear something in your little bakery," he said, his eyes holding mine.

The urge to roll my eyes was overwhelming, but I fought it, knowing it was early and I was cranky. I had only managed to get half a cup of coffee in my system. I'd need a lot more than that to deal with an interrogation. I was weary of his snooping around and his thinly veiled insinuations about my involvement with the accidental death at the factory.

"I'll make sure to keep my ears open," I replied politely.

With another glanced between us, he nodded. "Thanks," he mumbled, spun around and headed out the door.

It was then I noticed that he hadn't even bought a coffee.

"That was weird," Gabriel whispered.

"He's been acting strange for a couple of months now. I always feel like he's watching me. It creeps me out."

"What's creeping you out dear?" Lila said, pulling up a chair and sitting at our table.

It had taken a bit, but I was getting used to the complete lack of privacy in Lemon Bliss. It was a small town to begin with, but throw in my mother and her nosy friends and I could be almost guaranteed to have them show up wherever I happened to be. It wouldn't be a visit to the Crooked Coffee if someone didn't intrude on our quiet time together.

"Sheriff Smith," Gabriel answered. "He's practically been stalking Violet."

Lila shook her head. "He's been watching all of us a little too closely."

"It's just weird," I mumbled.

"Don't worry about it, and don't let him make you nervous. If you're nervous, you're more likely to slip up," she lectured.

Gabriel caught my eyes with a barely perceptible grin. Checking his watch, He announced it was time for him to go. He had a job in Ruby Red and would be out of town all day. He promised to call when he got back.

As soon as Gabriel left, Lila leaned in close. "You'll be there tonight?" she whispered.

"Yes. I don't have a choice, do I?"

She shook her head. "No, this is important."

"Is anybody else worried about Harold?" I asked.

The look on her face told me all I needed to know. "It is definitely worrisome, but I think I have a plan."

"What are you going to do, Lila?" I asked, afraid to know the answer.

She released a long sigh. "I'm going to cast a love spell."

"What does that mean?"

"I'm going to cast a spell to make him fall in love with me."

I gasped, "Lila!"

She shrugged a shoulder as if it was no big deal. "The spark is already there. It always has been. I'm just going to fan the flames a bit."

"Isn't that violating some rule?" I asked, shocked she was considering such a thing.

"It's for the good of the coven."

"How?"

"If Harold is in love with me, he'll be blinded to everything else. He won't be suspicious about who we are, because his focus will be on me. I'm taking one for the team," she grinned. "Besides, I've always been fond of Harold."

"Do the others know?" I asked, knowing my mother would likely not agree with her plan.

"I've told them my plan. They may not totally agree, but they know it's the only way to get the man to back off. He's like a dog with a bone! He won't let that business at the factory go. He's been snooping around and it's getting dangerous. We *all* need him to cool off a bit."

"I'm not going to argue with you there. I came home last week and he was at the house. He was just sitting in his truck, staring at grandma's flowers. It was very weird," I told her.

I shuddered, thinking of the scene. It had been unnerving, and it wasn't like I could call the cops and report that the sheriff was sitting in my driveway. Thankfully, he had left almost immediately. He had offered the excuse of wanting to see the flowers, but it didn't sit right with me. My spidey-sense had been tingling. I was beginning to trust that sixth sense a lot more now. I figured perhaps the fact I was a witch gave it a little more oomph. My mother swore it did.

She shook her head in disgust. "I blame that silly man, George whatever his name is. He needs to go away and leave us all alone," she said, referring to one of the supernatural investigators who'd been interested in the abandoned lemon tea factory bequeathed to me by my grandmother.

"Definitely. I can't say I'm happy to hear what you have to do, but I think you're right. It might be best for everyone. How long do you plan on keeping Harold under your spell?"

She waved a hand in the air. "I don't know. I guess until things settle down a bit."

"I have no business telling you what to do, but please be careful. Y'all have me a little freaked out about the repercussions of doing a spell. I don't want you to suffer any kind of negative consequences," I said with sincerity.

She was grinning. "Sweetie, we may have oversold the whole repercussions thing. Don't you worry about me."

"Just be careful."

"I will."

"I've got to get to work, Lila. Please be careful if you do go through with your plan. I'll see you tonight," I promised her, standing and getting ready to leave.

"I will. Keep your eyes and ears open. Things are about to get a little wild for us all," she warned. "Be cautious."

I eyed her, waiting for her to explain further, but she clearly had no intention of doing so. She was freaking me out. Were we in real danger? I needed to get to the bakery. Maybe Daphne would know more. If not, I would have to wait until tonight to find out why the museum break-in was so important to the coven. I could only imagine.

CHAPTER 3

*D*aphne and I approached the coven meeting that night with trepidation. Of course, it *had* to be held at midnight. I was trying to adjust to the rather astonishing fact I was a witch. Yet, the tendencies of the old guard witches—my mother and her friends—to be all cloak and dagger-ish were a bit ridiculous.

We both were tired after another exhausting day at the bakery and knew tomorrow would be a replay. We'd both attempted to hedge our way out of the meeting, but our respective mothers insisted. Given that we were still adjusting to the ways of being witches, we didn't feel it was wise to blow off the coven meeting. Especially not after my mother's worries about whatever had been stolen from the museum.

So there we were, driving out to the old lemon tea factory just before midnight. It had both of us on the cranky side.

"This sucks," Daphne mumbled, as we got out of the car at the factory. "I can't believe they're throwing such a big fit

over this museum thing. What do they expect us to do? Can't they cast a spell and make the items reappear?"

"Hopefully, it will be a quick meeting and we can get home and crawl into bed," I replied with a shrug.

On the heels of Daphne's sigh, we walked in the back-door, not bothering to let our eyes adjust to the blackness inside the factory. Daphne turned on her cellphone and we used the light to guide us to the secret door hidden by a magic spell. As we descended the stairs to the basement, we could hear the women talking. They were obviously in a heated discussion.

"Should we wait?" I whispered.

"No. I want to get this over with," she said, grumpily.

"We're here," I announced, stepping into the room.

All four women stopped their bickering and turned to look at us. My mother, Coral, Lila and Magnolia—four best friends, four witches and the women who'd finally coughed up their secret about our heritage a few months ago. Like me, Daphne had inherited her witchy ways from her mother Magnolia.

The women's faces were lined with tension and worry— all four of them. Sweet Jesus. I couldn't remember a time when I had seen my mother so concerned. She might be on the dramatic side, but it usually passed quickly.

"Finally," Coral grumped. "We were wondering how late you would be."

I opened my mouth to shoot back a retort, but stopped when my mother gave a gentle shake of her head. Coral was usually a very pleasant woman, and because she was Gabriel's aunt, I didn't really want to get on her bad side. Yet, I was in no mood to be lectured. We were a minute late. Unlike the four of them, Daphne and I had jobs.

"Have a seat ladies," Magnolia gestured to the seating area.

Daphne and I sat together on one of the couches, quietly

waiting for one of them to speak. After they'd fessed up and admitted this old lemon tea factory—bequeathed to me by my grandmother—had been the location for coven meetings for centuries, we'd found ourselves here every so often for meetings. Before the factory existed here, another home was in the same location with the same hidden doorway into this meeting room.

"What's this emergency meeting about?" I asked, encouraging them to get to the point.

"We have a situation," my mother started. "One that is very serious and needs to be addressed right away."

"The museum theft?" I prompted.

"Yes," Magnolia replied. "Two very precious items were stolen."

Daphne sighed loud enough for the entire room to hear. She was making her irritation known. I didn't blame her, but it wasn't helping matters.

"The two items stolen are important to our coven. They hold our secrets," Coral said from her seat in one of the bright purple wingback chairs. "Everything we are could be exposed."

"What items? If they were important to the coven, why were they left in the museum?" I asked, a little irritated to discover we were dealing with a situation that could have been prevented. "Why wouldn't they have been hidden here with the other items?"

Magnolia and Lila looked at each other before looking to my mom and Coral. Sweet tea, as my grandmother would have said. All this looking around without much to show for it.

"There's no good answer for that," my mother answered. "It isn't a choice the four of us made. Our mothers and grandmothers established that museum. They chose to hide the items in plain sight, and quite frankly, we never really worried about it. That is, until now."

"Okay. So, what we do now?" I asked.

Magnolia patted my mother on the shoulder. "It's okay, dear. We'll figure it out."

My mother appeared more upset by the missing items than the rest of them. I wondered if they were more personal to her, or if she had the most to lose. Curiosity warred with worry in my mind. I wasn't exactly thrilled to be sitting here, but I didn't want my mother to worry. I would protect her in any way I could.

"The missing items," Coral started, taking a deep breath. "One is a chest. Nothing fancy or anything like that, but it holds enchantments that are very important to our way of life."

"Enchantments?" Daphne asked.

"Yes, they are spells of sorts. Most of the enchantments in the box are there to help keep our coven safe. They were created more than two-hundred years ago when witches needed safe-guarding from those that were actively hunting and prosecuting anyone who even hinted at being a witch," my mother explained. "The box has been passed down through the generations. New enchantments were added over time."

"Virginia, tell them the other part," Lila said worriedly.

"The chest also holds evil enchantments," my mother announced. "It's an unusual practice, but our ancestors thought it would be best to keep everything together."

"Huh?" Daphne and I replied in unison and brilliantly, of course.

"I'm guessing that's bad," Daphne added with a quick grin in my direction.

"Very. If the wrong person were to open that chest, it would release evil into the world. Evil such as you have never seen before," Coral whispered. "Horrible evils. Witch lines that have had their powers bound because they prac-ticed the dark arts would be able to use their powers again."

Daphne suddenly seemed very concerned. "Do the bad witches know who we are? Will they use their dark magic against us?"

The four women looked at one another and then back at us. "It's possible. Our world is a fine balance of good and evil. Good witches and other beings have fought for centuries against those that are on the dark side. You could think of it as a war of sorts, and that chest holds some of the victories. Should the chest be opened and those enchantments released, not only would good witches be exposed, the dark arts would be infused with power."

I nodded, fighting back the panicky feeling building inside. To say I felt out of my depth was an understatement. Sweet tea! I was still getting used to being a witch. I'd talked myself into thinking it was okay with a focus on all the *good* a witch could do. I hadn't prepped myself for fending off dark arts and the like.

I had no idea what evil could be trapped in that box, but I believed them when they said it shouldn't be released. I'd seen more than enough movies about what could go wrong with that kind of thing.

"Okay. What do we do?" I asked, hoping there was a quick and easy solution. I couldn't imagine not being able to save the world. What good were powers if you couldn't use them in situations like this?

"Hold on. You don't know the whole story. Sadly, that's not the worst of it," my mother continued. "The other item stolen was an inkwell and pen."

I burst out with nervous laughter. "I can't even imagine what that thing can do."

My mother glared at me. "It's a very dangerous tool. It has the ability to read and write spells. Meaning, if it is in the wrong hands, it could be used as a weapon against us. It knows when spells have been cast as well. It threatens to expose us."

I shook my head. "I don't understand. How is that even possible? No, wait, never mind. Don't answer. Magic, right?"

"Yes, magic," she answered.

"Tell me again why such powerful items were left in the open, accessible to anyone?" I asked, not bothering to hide the frustration in my voice.

"The items are not technically ours to keep. We've known where they were and we've kept an eye on them. We don't need them and certainly don't want them, but we are responsible for keeping them out of the wrong hands."

"Who would take them? Do you think another witch would want them because she knows what they are?" Daphne asked.

"We don't know," Lila answered. "I can tell you the sheriff isn't all that concerned about the items. They hold no monetary value. He isn't even opening a formal investigation. He's too busy looking into that supernatural investigator's ridiculous story. It's up to us to find the items and put them away for safekeeping."

"Without anyone noticing what we're doing," my mother added, her tone laced with worry.

"And how are we going to do that?" I asked.

"We're not sure," Magnolia piped in.

Glancing around, I nodded. Now I understood why they were all so upset.

"Crap," I muttered, not excited to have another crisis hanging over my head. Where was that peaceful, laid-back lifestyle that was supposed to come with living in a small town?

"For now, we need to be very careful—no charming or spell casting," Magnolia said. "We don't know who has that inkwell. If it decides to reveal when a spell has been cast or magic has been used, we risk exposure."

My mother glanced between Daphne and me. "No more

practice spells. I know that will be a bit of a setback, but we'll pick up once all of this is settled."

I was a little bummed, but understood why it was necessary. Over the past couple months, they'd had been giving Daphne and I a crash course in witchcraft. I had found it very interesting, to say the least. Daphne and I had been having fun while learning. When it came to moving things, we had made a competition of it. Whoever could move something faster and farther was the winner. I was a little more proficient in that area, while Daphne seemed to be better at spell casting. My attempt to transform a wilting flower into a brilliant bloom resulted in it dying and the petals falling to the ground.

I had not inherited my grandmother's green thumb, even when it came to magical green thumbs. At least, so far that seemed to be the case. We were also learning the art of charming, which required a certain finesse. I tended to be a little heavy-handed in that department.

"Is there anything we can do?" I asked. "I mean, can we go on a search?"

"We all need to be actively looking," Lila added.

"How do we know what we're looking for?" Daphne asked.

Excellent question. An inkwell and a chest were pretty generic descriptions.

My mom and Lila exchanged a look. "The chest is old. Really old. It's made of wood and has some ornate designs carved into the lid. The lock is black iron," Lila explained.

"And the inkwell?" I asked, not even sure I knew what an inkwell was.

"Look it up online," Coral snarked. "It's pretty standard, nothing fancy."

When Daphne made a sound, I stopped her. We were both tired and cranky. The elder witches were stressed and frustrated.

"I think we all need to go home and get some sleep. We'll all look for the chest and inkwell and refrain from magic. Does that sum it all up?" I said, yawning.

Everyone looked at one another before we all agreed to go home for the night. Daphne and I left first, knowing the others wanted to talk without us present. That was all well and good. I was too tired to care.

"Can you believe that?" Daphne said, once we were inside my car. "An old chest that holds enchantments. I mean, they're talking like it's Pandora's box."

"Do you think that's real?" I asked.

"I don't know. I just want to go home, go to bed and worry about mystery chests and inkwells tomorrow," she said, leaning her head back.

CHAPTER 4

$\mathcal{T}$he following day was another busy one after the coven meeting. Daphne and I were both exhausted after our late night, but the fear of evil looming energized us. I had baked and baked and baked some more. We were gearing up for the weekend, leaving us no time to chat about what our mothers had told us.

During a lull in the afternoon, Daphne drifted into the kitchen. I leaned against the baking counter in the back and took a gulp from my now-cold coffee.

"Hanging in there?" I asked, taking in her slightly disheveled appearance.

She nodded and yawned. "Yes. I'm going to bed at seven tonight. I don't care if that makes me old. I am absolutely beat. I don't think I realized how much work this would be."

"It will get better," I told her with a smile. "We'll get into a groove and soon this will be an average day."

She giggled, "If you say so."

"I do. Have you talked to your mom at all today?" I asked, bringing up the delicate subject.

"No. You?"

I shook my head. "Nope. I figured they would have come by. Maybe they're going to gang up on us at the end of the day."

"It really is a mess. Half of me, the part that still doesn't truly believe in all the supernatural, thinks they are totally overreacting. The other half of me is scared to death. When I finally managed to get to sleep last night, all I could think about was evil spirits taking over our little town of Lemon Bliss. I imagined goblins and demons and every other horrible creature I've read about in books or seen in movies," she said.

"I know the feeling. I'm familiar with the struggle. I'm still a little angry we're even dealing with this in the first place. Why wouldn't they do a better job securing such dangerous tools of the dark side?"

"I don't know. They deserve to be grounded," she mumbled.

I chuckled and finished off my cold coffee. Us grounding our own mothers wasn't something I had ever thought would be necessary, but in this situation, I agreed with her. They'd totally screwed up leaving those artifacts in plain sight, and now we were all facing some potentially serious ramifications.

The jingling of the bells above the door out front pulled Daphne out of the kitchen to deal with a new round of customers. I finished up with the frosting on the fresh batch of cupcakes and carried them out front. I was pleased to see all the small tables filled with local kids from the high school. They weren't the cleanest customers, but their money was as green as anyone else's. As customers, they tended to multiply. One or two happy customers quickly became ten in the blink of an eye. In the time it took to send a text message, one small sale turned into a rush.

"Did they all buy something?" I asked in amazement.

Daphne smiled and nodded. "They did. Can you imagine

if we would have had a bakery in town when we were in high school? We would have been huge!"

I laughed. "And broke. All of our hard-earned allowance would have been spent on cookies."

We casually watched as the group of teens tore through their cookies and muffins. They were all chatting and laughing with each other. My ears perked up at a comment.

"Did he just say something about the museum?" I hissed.

She nodded her head, eyes wide. Both of us pretended to be busy stocking and wiping down the case while we listened intently.

The group got a little rowdy as they talked about who would want anything from that dusty old museum. There was a football game coming up and they tossed around the idea the museum may have been broken into by the rival team.

"Joke's on them. There's nothing in there but a bunch of old stuff no one cares about," one of the boys laughed. "What morons. We should go see if they have a museum."

There plunged into a plan to get revenge on the other team. I debated with myself about intervening, but quickly decided against it. Let their mothers deal with them.

"Are they seriously going to pee in the town's fountain?" Daphne asked, when all the teens had left the bakery.

I looked at her and rolled my eyes. "I think so. I mean, they're teenage boys. Peeing on things is kinda par for the course. Remind me to never dip my toes in that fountain."

"Do you think they were right? That the guys on that other football team broke in and stole the stuff?"

I shrugged a shoulder. "I don't know. It seems kind of stupid, but then again, peeing in a fountain isn't exactly brilliant. Have you heard anything else from any of the other customers?"

"Most of the folks I casually asked about it had the same idea. They all think it was a silly prank pulled by some bored kids. The rival football team is a new twist on it that I hadn't heard." She smiled. "Wouldn't it be funny if the chest and inkwell were sitting in some stinky boy's room, buried under a pile of dirty laundry?"

I laughed. "Yes. Hopefully, if that's the case, someone's parents will turn it in. Crisis averted."

"Could we be so lucky?"

I shook my head. "I don't know. It doesn't make sense to me. I wonder if anything else was taken? I mean, if it was only the chest and inkwell, I think we have to assume it is someone who knew what those items truly were."

"I agree. Why isn't Harold doing anything about it? A theft is a theft, even if it isn't a big deal in his eyes. What else could he possibly be doing? Lemon Bliss and the surrounding towns aren't exactly a hotbed of crime," she said, rolling her eyes.

I laughed. "Oh, that reminds me. I forgot to tell you about Lila's plan."

"Lila has a plan to get the chest back?"

"No, no. Harold isn't looking into the museum theft because he's too busy looking into us, or the idea there is a supernatural presence here in Lemon Bliss."

Daphne nodded. "And Lila has a plan to do what exactly?"

"Distract him," I said with a grin. "She's going to cast a love spell to make him fall in love with her. She thinks if he's busy chasing her, he isn't going to be quite so interested in following up on that supernatural investigation."

"I thought we weren't supposed to cast any spells with that inkwell on the loose?" she asked, her eyes wide.

"Lila thinks it's a good bet. As much as I think it's a bad idea, it may be necessary, especially now," I reasoned.

"I thought our lives would get easier," Daphne complained. "Finding out I was a witch was supposed to be a good thing."

"Tell me about it." With a shake of my head, I spun away. "I should get back in the kitchen and try to get a jump start on what we need for tomorrow."

"Looks like you have a visitor," she said.

Glancing back, I caught her sly grin. My gaze traveled past her to look out the large windows facing the street. I smiled when I saw Gabriel walking by with a tray of coffees in his hand.

"He's definitely worth keeping if he brings you coffee every day," she murmured as Gabriel pushed open the door.

"Hi!" I greeted, a little hum of joy buzzing through me.

"Hey there. I thought you ladies could use a little pick-me-up," he said, as he set the tray on the counter.

"For me, too?" Daphne asked, her tone surprised.

"Of course," he said, flashing a smile.

She turned to me with a grin. "Definitely a keeper."

Gabriel laughed. "Guess what I just found out?"

I was afraid to guess since this week was already off to a rocky start.

"What?" Daphne moaned. "No more bad news."

"I don't know if it's bad news, but I don't think it's good news."

"What's wrong?" I asked.

"Remember that supernatural investigator? Not the one who died, but his partner."

Daphne and I nodded in unison. "Yes," I said, waiting for him to reveal what I could already tell was going to be bad news.

"He's back."

I groaned. Daphne gasped and then cursed under her breath.

"How do you know?" I asked.

"I ran into him at the hardware store. He was picking up some plastic. I played nice and found out he's renting Old Man Harrison's cabin," he explained.

I knew the place. It was several miles outside of town. The cabin had been lived in by the man I'd only knew as Old Man Harrison back when I was in school. It had sat empty for years, and I would have thought it would have fallen in on itself by now.

"Great," Daphne mumbled.

Neither one of us mentioned the missing items from the museum.

"Anyway, I thought you should know. Be careful, ladies," he warned. "I've got to get back to work. I just wanted to stop by, say hello and bring you some coffee."

"I'll walk you out," I said, taking off my apron.

"Sorry to be the bearer of bad news," he started as we pushed through the door and out front. "I know what his presence in town meant last time. I have a feeling he isn't letting the story go."

"I agree. I'll talk to my mom tonight and let her know. I doubt any of them are going to be all that pleased to hear he's back. I hope Harold doesn't get caught up in whatever that guy is up to," I said, knowing it was probably too late for that.

It explained why Harold had been asking so many questions. Lila's love spell was more important than ever now. We had to get the sheriff disinterested in whatever George was investigating. I'd never thought I'd be worried about supernatural investigators, but when this town had more than its share of witches who had supernatural powers and I happened to be one of them, well, the idea went from half-baked to scary.

"I'll call you tonight, unless you have another meeting," Gabriel offered when we paused by his car.

"Not yet, but I have a feeling once the rest of them find out George is back, there's a good chance we'll be called in for another meeting."

"Good luck," he said, before climbing in his truck and driving off.

I walked into the bakery to find Daphne on the phone. Judging by her side of the conversation, I could tell she was talking to her mother, Magnolia.

"Yep, another meeting tonight," she announced before I had to ask the question.

I groaned, "I'm never going to catch up on my sleep."

"I think we know why those items went missing," she stated.

"Why won't that man just go away? I don't understand what he hopes to prove."

She shrugged a shoulder. "He wants to prove to the world that witches exist right here in Louisiana."

"I'm going to get started baking. I have a feeling I'm not going to want to get up early tomorrow."

"What if he opened the chest?" Daphne asked.

That was the very question that had been on my mind since Gabriel announced George was back in town.

"I don't know. I hope our mentors have some ideas," I said tiredly. "It could still be a prank and his return to Lemon Bliss nothing more than a coincidence."

She guffawed. "Yeah, right!"

"Way to think positive!" I yelled from the kitchen as I pushed through the swinging door.

Her laughter followed me. I wasn't about to fall into the rabbit hole of doom and gloom. Not yet. I wanted to hold onto hope that there was a way out of this mess. After all, we managed to get through the last crisis relatively unscathed. My mom and her friends would think of something. I hoped.

CHAPTER 5

That evening, as Daphne and I worked together to clean up the kitchen, a question kept kicking the tires in the back of my mind. Unsure whether I should ask, I finally decided I might as well. If anyone would understand, it would be Daphne. She was in the same boat as me, a decidedly strange boat to boot.

The chances of stumbling across anyone else in the whole wide world who belatedly learned they happened to be a witch were slim to none. Every time my mind processed this astonishing turn of events, I wondered if I'd wake up the next day and realize it was all a crazy dream.

Like me, Daphne had recently moved back to Lemon Bliss. She'd returned to our old hometown after her marriage hit the skids, and I'd been called back after the mysterious death at the factory. We'd each decided to stay and were hoping to learn more about who and what we were.

"Daphne," I said, taking a deep breath.

"Hmm," she murmured as she carefully covered cookies with plastic wrap.

"Do you think I should tell Gabriel about the chest and what it is?"

"I don't know. That could be risky."

"You think? I mean, he knows we're witches. He knows his aunt is a witch, and he knows about the coven and our meetings. It doesn't seem like it's that risky to explain to him why the chest and inkwell are so important," I reasoned.

She was quiet for several minutes. "Personally, I think he can be trusted, but I think you should ask your mom. I don't know how much they ever told any of their husbands."

"I had a feeling you would say that. I hate keeping secrets from him."

"How serious are things getting with you two anyway?" she asked.

"I'm not sure, but can they ever really get serious if I'm hiding something this big from him? I don't want a relationship based on secrets and lies."

A bitter smile twisted her lips. "Trust me, you really don't. I'm still dealing my ex. I wished I would have known who he was before I married him. Our entire relationship was nothing but secrets and lies."

"I'm sorry. How are things going with the divorce?" I asked. I knew she'd filed and the process was taking time, but it was a sore subject, so I tried not to bring it up too often.

"Slow. He's doing his damnedest to make everything far more difficult than it needs to be."

I heard a quacking sound coming from the front of the bakery. "What's that?"

Daphne started giggling. "That would be my phone."

"It quacks?" I asked in confusion.

She looked at me and winked. "That's my mom's ringtone."

I burst out laughing. "You better hope she never hears

34

herself calling you. I have a feeling she would be less than thrilled with being designated a quack."

"You should hear the ringtone for my ex," she said, walking through the swinging door to the front of the bakery.

Daphne was gone several minutes before she returned, her shoulders slumped.

"What's wrong?" I asked with concern.

"You don't want to know."

I wrinkled my nose. I sensed what she was going to say, but had to ask anyway. "Let me guess, they want to meet at midnight again?"

With a sigh, she nodded.

"Did you tell her about George being back in town?"

"No, I didn't even get a chance to. She was rambling on and on. We can tell them tonight."

"We're going to be dragging butt tomorrow. Two nights in a row is rough."

"Agreed. I'm gonna go home and take a nap. I'll pick you up this time," she said.

Glancing around the kitchen, I ascertained we could call it good for the evening. Walking out together, I waved goodbye as Daphne pulled out of the parking lot.

Once I got back to my grandmother's house, which I was still struggling to accept as my home, I decided to follow Daphne's lead and take a power nap.

I woke to in a state of confusion to my alarm going off. Getting up when it was prime sleeping time made no sense to my tired body, but I dragged myself out of bed. I threw on a pair of jeans and headed downstairs to wait for Daphne.

Within minutes, she was honking her horn. We'd learned the hard way that our fellow witches did not appreciate tardiness.

"Did you get any sleep?" I asked, getting into her car.

"Some. James called and wanted to fight."

"Why do you bother answering his calls? Block his damn number," I said firmly. We had gone over this before. Her ex-husband wouldn't leave her alone and seemed intent on making her life miserable.

"I was hoping he would sign the papers if I played nice," she grumbled. "I should have known that wasn't in his DNA."

When we arrived at the factory, Lila was just getting out of her car. "Hello, dears. I'm so sorry we have to keep pulling you out of your warm beds after working so hard all day."

"Thank you, Lila. It's nice to hear that someone under-stands," I replied, feeling a little better about the midnight rendezvous.

We walked in together and found the other three women were already in the basement room.

"We did a locator spell!" my mom blurted out.

"I thought we weren't supposed to use magic or cast any spells?" Daphne asked.

"The situation warranted the risk," Magnolia answered. "We found the chest!"

"You did?" I asked in surprise. "That's good, right? So now all we have to worry about is the inkwell? The inkwell isn't evil, which means the danger has passed?"

The look on my mother's face told me that was not the case at all. "We know where the chest is, but we don't have it, and we don't know who does."

"Where is it?" Daphne asked.

"At a house outside of town," Magnolia said. "The old Harrison property."

Daphne and I looked at each other.

"Oh no," I groaned.

"Yes, but at least we know where it's at," my mom said hopefully.

"No, it isn't that. George Cannon, the supernatural investigator, he's renting Old Man Harrison's cabin."

There was a collective gasp in the room.

Daphne jumped in to explain. This news was not good, and I watched the color drain from the women's faces as the information sank in.

"We have to get it back," Magnolia said, in a determined voice. "We have no idea what that man may do. If he finds a way to open that chest..." Her words trailed off, letting the threat hang in the air.

"How?" I asked. "Can we ask him for it?"

"We can't just knock on his door and ask him. He'll want to know how we knew he had it," Coral reasoned.

"What if one of us went out there?" I asked.

Lila laughed. "The man knows we don't like him. I think he may be a little suspicious if we showed up out there."

"We have to do something!" Coral exclaimed, desperation in her voice.

The room fell quiet. Going near George was risky. He didn't know who we were, but he knew there was something magical about Lemon Bliss. I didn't know much about supernatural items, but I couldn't help but wonder if he had some kind of radar or device that cued him when an object had powers. Maybe I was being paranoid, and I could recognize that possibility, but I was terrified. The idea that he could set dark powers loose—sweet tea, we had problems.

"I don't think there is any way we can safely show up at the man's front door and ask for the chest. Maybe we should stake the place out. When he leaves, we go in. One of us keeps watch while the others look for it," I offered.

"That could work," Magnolia said. "Anyone else have any ideas?"

"Isn't there a spell we can use to have the chest come to us?" Daphne asked.

"It's too risky," Coral said, right away.

Catching Daphne's eye, I elected to remain silent on the fact they'd already used a spell to locate the damn thing.

"Virginia, what do you think?" Magnolia asked my mother.

She looked down at her hands. "I think we need to take a day and try to find out why George is in Lemon Bliss again. Lila, how is Harold?"

Lila giggled like a school girl. "Harold is quite fine."

"Do you think you could ask him if he knows anything about George's return?"

"I'll try, but I don't see why he would. I didn't get the idea he liked the man, or cared for his nosing around Lemon Bliss when they were here last time," she replied.

"I have a question, and I hope all of you will have an open mind," I started. "I need to know how much I can tell Gabriel about the missing artifacts."

"Nothing!" Magnolia said so loudly I nearly jumped off the couch.

"Why not? He knows we're witches. He knows we meet here. Why can't I talk with him about this?"

My mother came to sit beside me, resting one of her hands on my knee. "Dear, it isn't that we don't trust him. We do. We know he would never reveal our secrets. It isn't that at all."

"Then, what is it?" I asked, not understanding why they were so against it.

"It's far too dangerous," Coral said. "We keep him in the dark to protect him. The more he knows, the more danger he's in."

I didn't understand. "How could it be dangerous?"

Coral spoke in a gentle voice. "If someone knew our secret and knew that Gabriel knew, but was helpless to protect himself, it would be far too risky. We also have to consider the burden we carry. Is it fair to put that on

Gabriel's shoulders? His mother told him far more than she should have. I enjoyed being able to talk freely around him, but it's selfish."

I shook my head. "I don't believe that. He's genuinely interested and concerned. Gabriel can take care of himself," I said, a little too tersely.

"That's exactly why we have to protect him," Coral replied. "He's fiercely loyal. What if this chest or the inkwell exposes us? Gabriel would be prosecuted right along with us, when he's truly innocent."

"Oh, I didn't think of that," I said, feeling deflated. I wasn't loving this whole secrets thing.

Coral smiled and nodded her head. "I know it's hard, and maybe one day it will be safe to reveal all of our secrets, but for now, we need to keep him out of as many of our troubles as we can."

"Okay, okay. I won't say anything," I promised.

"Alright then, everyone, go home and do your best to get some rest. I'll see what information I can glean from Harold," Lila said, clapping her hands together.

"We'll see what else we can learn from gossip around the bakery," Daphne said, yawning and stretching.

"Maybe that George character will show up for a muffin or something," Magnolia muttered. "If he does, call me right away and I'll go out to that cabin and find that chest, and hopefully the inkwell, too. That man is a menace."

"I agree," Coral said. "We'll get the chest and then we will figure out a way to chase him out of Lemon Bliss for good."

I didn't even want to think about what she was planning. This was what she really meant about keeping Gabriel in the dark. She didn't want to make him an accomplice. I wasn't so sure I wanted to be an accomplice myself.

We gradually filtered out of the room.

"Let's go," Daphne said, waiting at the stairs.

I went, but not before looking back at the four women

watching us. I felt as if we were on the precipice of something big. A twinge of fear coiled up my spine, causing a shudder to run through me.

"Are you okay?" Daphne whispered.

"Fine, just one of those weird feelings," I mumbled.

"I don't think it is a feeling. I think it's a premonition," she said as we climbed the stairs to leave.

I sensed she was right.

CHAPTER 6

"No, not again," I groaned, looking at the digital display on my alarm clock.

Closing my eyes, I willed the numbers to change. I didn't want it to be time to get up already. Not yet. I was so tired, I felt like I needed to sleep for a week. Last night after Daphne dropped me off, I hadn't been able to fall asleep. I couldn't get past the feeling of something lurking in the dark. I didn't know if it was due to the way the others had been acting, or if it was my sixth sense that seemed to be in overdrive. No matter what it was, it was making me a little crazy.

What finally dragged me out of bed was Gabriel. We were meeting for coffee again this morning. I couldn't wait to see him, even if I couldn't tell him about anything that was going on. Though I'd accepted and understood the reasoning behind not filling him in, it still wasn't sitting well with me. The secrets and shady behavior were not my style. I preferred to be brutally honest. It made things much simpler.

When I walked into Crooked Coffee, I scanned the room

to find Gabriel already seated, chatting with an elderly woman who seemed to be enjoying the attention. My heart gave a little thump. He was kind, caring and just a genuinely good guy. I couldn't unburden myself of secrets at his expense.

"Hey!" he said, waving me over when he saw me standing near the door.

With a smile, I walked towards him. "Hey, yourself. I see you're charming all the ladies."

The woman giggled and winked. "He's all yours, honey."

"You know me, a real ladies man," he offered with a wry grin. "Here's your coffee."

"Thank you," I said, curling my hand around the cup and sliding into the chair across from him.

His gaze coasted over my face. "You had another meeting last night, didn't you?"

Momentarily, I considered playing stupid or lying, but I couldn't do it. "Yes."

"Want to tell me what's going on?"

I smiled. "Nothing. You know the ladies. They tend to get worked up over nothing."

He didn't believe me. I could see the skepticism in his gaze. "They do, but you normally don't."

I shrugged a shoulder. "I'm not worked up."

"The dark circles under your eyes say otherwise. Did you sleep at all last night?"

"I'm fine, really. I'm just a little tired."

"Come on, what' up? Tell me and maybe I can help you sort it out. Two heads are better than one, right?" he said with a friendly smile.

"It's no big deal," I said, hoping I sounded convincing.

Cocking his head to the side, he eyed me. "I know something is up. Aunt Coral is an absolute wreck. She keeps telling me she's okay, but I know she's lying. There is something big happening in your world and neither of you trusts me enough to tell me."

I didn't say anything. What could I say? If I told him nothing was wrong again, he would know I was lying. Lacking the mental strength to get into an argument, I bailed instead, cutting our coffee date short.

"I need to run by the post office and then get to the bakery. Thanks for the coffee. I owe you a week's worth of coffee at least. Maybe you'll let me pay you back with a cherry pie or a dozen chocolate chip muffins?" I asked with a grin.

"Don't worry about it," he said.

I stood up, debating with myself about apologizing, and finally deciding against it. I needed to figure out what to tell him. He wasn't going to accept a simple answer.

"I'll call you tonight," I told him.

With a nod, he took a sip of his coffee. We were conveniently interrupted when his phone rang. He took the call before quickly saying goodbye. I took my cue to leave.

Walking through the coffee shop, I pushed through the doors into the adjacent post office. Heading to the back where my box was located, I pulled out my mail and sifted through it quickly.

A pair of male voices caught my attention. I recognized one of the voices right away, but the other didn't ring a bell. I casually changed my position by a few feet, so I could see around the corner. It was Harold talking to the man I knew to be George Cannon. I pretended to be interested in my mail and leaned up against the corner. They were in a rather heated discussion. I couldn't quite make out what they were saying, so I moved towards the table positioned against a far wall, within hearing distance of them.

"I didn't do it," George hissed. "It just showed up. I don't know what I'm supposed to do with it."

Harold's back was to me, but I could tell by his posture

he was tense. "Like I believe that. I told you I would take care of things here. I don't need you stirring up trouble."

"Ha, as if you could handle anything. You don't even know what you're looking for," George said, in a low voice. "This is my job. I'm not letting this story go."

"I'm the sheriff around here. I know these people. No one is going to talk to you. I suggest you figure out a way to get that thing back where it belongs. These folks aren't going to appreciate a thief living in their town," Harold whispered. "Don't make me arrest you."

"Who you calling a thief? I told you I didn't take it. Someone is setting me up."

"I'm telling you, put it back. I don't know why you took it in the first place." Harold was clearly frustrated.

"I told you, I didn't take it. Someone left it for me," George insisted.

Harold scoffed. "You expect me to believe that chest just magically showed up on your front porch?"

"Yes! That's exactly what I expect you to believe, because that's exactly what happened," George practically shouted.

Glancing around, I noticed I wasn't the only one watching them. The postal worker was as well. I got the feeling she was also watching me. I met her eyes and defiantly glared back, surprised when she didn't back down.

Harold noticed the postal worker. I saw him turning to follow her gaze and quickly looked down at my mail, pretending to be absorbed in whatever bill was in my hand.

"Violet," he said.

I looked up to see George looking straight at me, a startled look on his face.

"Good morning, Sheriff," I said, with a pleasant smile.

"I need to get going," George said, quickly escaping the post office. He shot me one last look before darting out the door.

"How's the bakery going?" Harold asked, closing the gap between us.

"Great actually. It's been very busy," I said. Harold had been making me nervous as of late, and I was afraid he was going to ask me about the museum theft.

"Has Lila been by there a lot?" he asked, and I could see the twinkle in his eye. I had never asked Lila if she had followed through with her plan, but judging by the way Harold was asking, he was definitely under her spell.

"Nope, I haven't seen her, but I do spend most of my time in the back kitchen area. Have you been by, yet?" I asked.

He looked a little embarrassed. "No, I've been busy. I haven't spent a lot of time in town during the day. When I get back, you're already closed up."

I smiled. "No worries, we'll be around. You'll have plenty of time to stop in."

His gaze held mine, and I sensed he was sizing me up. Maybe it was in my head, but it always made me squirm. It was my guilt making me crazy. There was no possible way he knew I was a witch, or that there were quite a few others floating around Lemon Bliss. At least, that was what I told myself.

"Maybe I'll come by today. I'll see if Lila would like to go with me and try some of those cookies I've been hearing so much about."

"That'd be great. I've got to run. The morning rush is a busy one, and I've got to get started on those cookies," I said. With a smile, I slipped my mail in my purse and hurried out.

As I left, I looked back to see the woman behind the counter still staring at me. I chalked it up to curiosity, but something told me she didn't like me. I didn't know why, but it was a feeling I couldn't shake. I didn't recognize her.

I needed to talk to the ladies about what I'd overheard in

the post office. George definitely had the chest and Harold knew about it. That created several more questions. Why hadn't Harold taken the chest back and returned it to the museum? George seemed adamant he hadn't actually stolen the chest, which was odd. Either man could have given it back, but neither seemed to be inclined to do it. Why would anyone put a stolen chest on George's porch? That made no sense at all.

Arriving at the bakery, I got started with my morning tasks. Baking helped me think. I ran through the many scenarios that could explain the missing chest and just how Harold and George were involved. The way they'd been talking implied they had somewhat of a familiar relationship. I didn't realize the men were friends or even acquaintances. That worried me. The last thing we needed was an overzealous supernatural investigator buddying up to the town sheriff. I really needed to talk to my mom.

When Daphne came in, I quickly told her what I had overheard.

"I say we tell the others and let them go through with their plan to steal it back," she said immediately.

I nodded slowly, worries still running laps in my mind. "Maybe George will come in here and we could keep an eye on him while Mom and the others get that chest back. Can you believe he said someone left it on his porch?" I asked with exasperation.

Daphne giggled. "If I got caught with stolen merchandise, I'd probably say the same thing. Plead innocent."

"I don't know. Why do you think Harold hasn't taken it back, though? Doesn't that seem odd to you?" This detail had been puzzling me all morning.

"Maybe Harold is the one who put it on his porch," she offered.

"Setting him up?"

Daphne shrugged. "Or hoping he would know what it was and what to do with it."

"Do you think Harold knows that it's charmed?"

She sighed. "Nothing would surprise me. We know Harold has been doing a lot of snooping around. Maybe he found out the inkwell and the chest were magical."

"Who would ever accuse the sheriff of stealing? It's the perfect crime," I said.

"He stole the items, but didn't know what to do with them, so he took them to the supernatural expert, hoping he would know what to do," Daphne offered.

I started laughing. It was all too ridiculous to be true, but the reality of my life lately was that anything too ridiculous *was* true.

"We'll have to worry about it later," I said, brushing away my witch worries until after we closed for the day. "For now, let's worry about getting through another hectic day on very little sleep."

Daphne grabbed her cash drawer and headed out front. It wasn't long before I heard the bell above the door jingling. I didn't get time to stress about magic chests and inkwells for the next eight hours.

CHAPTER 7

inally, a day off from the bakery and I couldn't have been happier. Actually, that wasn't quite right. Finally, I had slept in and felt refreshed. The day before had been our busiest yet. Daphne and I had decided we shouldn't wait a full month before hiring help after all. We needed it sooner rather than later. We were actually losing money by not being able to serve our customers fast enough.

All of that could wait. Today, we had other priorities. We had hatched a plan to do a little investigating on our own. The rest of the coven was in the dark. They were still worried about how they were going to get the chest from George. Now that we knew where it was, we could rest a little easier. The assumption was he also had the inkwell.

George hadn't returned either item to the museum, which led us to believe he was keeping them as part of his supernatural investigation. It was a dangerous weapon, but my mom and the others weren't convinced he knew exactly how dangerous. The plan was to get the items back before he did.

After showering, getting dressed and enjoying a cup of coffee, I called Daphne.

"You ready?" I asked.

"Yep. Do you want to pick me up?"

"Sure, I'll be right over."

I called Gabriel, but he didn't answer. I had a feeling he was still frustrated with me. When I'd called last night, he'd again tried to prod about what was going on. When I'd again dodged his questions, he'd been polite, but I sensed his frustration. I figured he needed a little time and didn't pressure him. Once I was done with Daphne today, I would call him again.

"This should be fun," Daphne said, getting into the car when I pulled up in front of her place.

I laughed. "I don't know about fun, but I'm hoping to get some answers."

"I haven't been to the museum since we were kids."

"Me either. I wonder if there's anything new in it."

"I doubt it, unless there's something from your grand-mother." Seeing as my grandmother was the most recent witch to pass away, I supposed she could have donated something to the museum, but I sure hoped not.

We parked in front of the old Lemon Bliss museum and quickly signed up for the first tour of the day. The museum was only open a couple of hours. There were already several tourists signed up, which was a good thing for us. We needed to blend in.

"Ready?" I asked, pulling my baseball cap on.

Daphne took one look at me and burst out laughing. "Are you seriously wearing a hat?"

"Yes! Aren't you? What if someone recognizes us?"

She was still laughing. "For starters, it's just a baseball hat. It's not like anyone who knows you can't tell it's you. Also, what are they going to do? We're visiting the museum. It isn't exactly against the law."

"You and I both know we aren't just visiting."

"Well, I didn't bring a hat. I guess if they bust me, they bust me. You can bail me out of the non-existent jail."

"Don't take me down with you," I quipped.

We cased the place and were very pleased to see there was only one elderly lady running the show. It would be very easy to slip away and do our own snooping.

When she started talking, I leaned over to whisper to Daphne. "Let's go in the back and see if we can find the security tapes."

She looked at me like I was crazy. "Security tapes?"

I nodded and casually pointed up. "Look, there are cameras."

Her mouth dropped open. "Wow. When did that happen? I didn't think this place was a target for thieves. I can't believe they have cameras."

When the small group began to move towards the kitchen area, Daphne and I managed to slip away. "Where's the office?" I asked, not familiar with the museum's layout.

"Back there I assume."

We made our way around a few tables with displays laid out. "There," I said pointing to a room that had a sign stating only employees were allowed entry.

Daphne tried the door handle. It was locked. "Now what?" she asked in frustration.

I looked around, realizing we didn't have a lot of time. The museum wasn't that big. The group would be back before we knew it.

"Shh," I whispered before closing my eyes and concentrating on the locked door.

"What are you doing? Oh no. You better not be doing what I think you're doing," she warned.

I reached out and turned the door handle. "I did."

She shook her head. "You are going to be in so much trouble."

I shrugged. "What's the point of being a witch if I can never use my powers. We needed in here and this is important. A tiny bit of magic isn't going to matter," I reasoned. I'd been practicing my powers at home and discovered unlocking doors came pretty easy.

"Tell that to your mother," she said, walking into the dark office ahead of me.

I followed behind her and quietly shut the door before locking it, just in case someone else tried to come in. We got right to work searching the office.

"I found it. Look," I whispered, pointing to the bookshelf filled with tapes.

It was an outdated security system, but that was to be expected. I couldn't imagine the museum using digital anything. It just felt wrong.

"Do we take them?" she asked.

"Yep. We need a bag or something. How are we going to get these out of here without being seen?" I asked, realizing we were very unprepared. Clearly, we weren't thieves by nature, or we'd have planned better. I ignored the guilt nudging my conscience. This was for the greater good. If the chest was opened and the dark powers set loose, we'd have far more to worry about than a few stolen security tapes from a tiny museum.

"We should have thought this through a little more," Daphne mumbled.

I glanced around the room. "We'll toss them out the window and then pick them up."

She raised an eyebrow. "Which direction is the window facing? Don't you think someone will notice us tossing stuff out?"

I pulled back the curtain and looked into the alley. I turned and smiled. "It faces the alley. No one is going to notice. Come on. We have to hurry."

52

"I don't like this," she hissed. "What if there's an alarm on the window?"

"I guess we're about to find out," I said, unlocking the window and sliding it open.

We both waited, neither of us breathing or moving. When we didn't hear anything, I popped the screen out.

"Here," she said, handing me a few tapes.

"Look for a bag or a box," I ordered.

She emptied out a paper grocery sack. "This is it."

I stuffed some tapes inside and dropped it out the window, hoping the cassettes didn't break. "Grab the rest."

Daphne started dropping videotapes out the window. When the shelf was cleared, we looked at each other. "That may be a little obvious," she mused.

I shrugged my shoulders. "Oh well."

"Let's find the VCR. We need to pull the tape that's recording right now."

I started laughing. "You're right, duh. I didn't even think about that."

We spent several frantic minutes looking for the system and finally found it tucked into a small closet. Daphne ejected the tape and stuck it down her shirt.

I looked at her. "What are you doing?"

"I'm not letting the evidence of our breaking and entering get away from me. This one stays with me."

I nodded, relieved she was thinking on her feet. "You're kind of scaring me. You really think like a criminal."

She smiled and winked. "You can thank me later when you're not rotting in jail."

"Let's get out of here. I'll check and see if the group is back yet."

I slowly opened the door a crack, listening for voices.

"I think they're upstairs," she whispered. "Listen and you can hear the footsteps."

I paused. At the sound of footsteps above, I nodded. "Let's go."

We walked out of the office, locking the door behind us. We were going to make a break for it, but the group came downstairs at that exact moment.

"Everyone, please do sign the visitor's log. We love to see where people come from," the tour guide said. "There are souvenirs for sale along the back wall."

Daphne and I did our best to appear enthused as we looked at the souvenirs for sale. "I want to see that visitor's log," I whispered.

She nodded. "We'll snag it too."

"No! Let's just look back at who has signed in. Sheesh, you are seriously making me wonder about your past, Daphne."

She giggled. "You're the one who broke into a locked office."

"That's not the same thing," I argued.

"It's exactly the same thing."

We pretended to be signing our names. I used my body to shield Daphne as she flipped through the pages. "There's nothing here. I doubt a thief is actually going to sign in."

"You're right, let's get out of here before I throw up."

The moment we were outside, I sucked in the fresh air. I was not cut out to be a criminal. I was way too stressed out. Greater good or not, this made me anxious.

"Come on, we have to get those tapes before anyone sees them back there or the lady notices they're missing."

"Let me grab a bag out of my car. I don't want to be traipsing down the alley carrying the evidence in plain sight," I told her dashing towards my car.

Daphne followed me, slipping the cassette that had been in her shirt under the front passenger seat.

I grabbed a couple of the reusable shopping bags I kept in my car. I tossed one at her as we walked a block down the street before casually heading into the alley. Once we were out of sight, we ran towards the pile of videotapes and hurriedly stuffed them in the bags.

We strolled down the street towards my car, acting like it was the most normal thing in the world. Once we were safely inside the car, I started it up and raced down the road.

"Relax, no one is chasing you," Daphne said with a chuckle.

I slowed down. "I can't help it. That was intense. I kept waiting to get caught."

"We didn't. Now, what are we going to do with all of these tapes?"

"We watch them, but first I need more coffee."

She burst into laughter. "The last thing you need is coffee. Look at you. You're so jumpy already, a cup of coffee will give you the jitters."

"I'm not jumpy and I need coffee," I shot back.

"Whatever you say, but I don't want to leave these tapes in here. I'll wait while you go in."

"Good idea."

"Violet," she started. "How are we going to watch these tapes? I don't have a VCR. No one does."

I smiled. "I do. Let's just say these aren't the first security tapes I've stolen since I've been in Lemon Bliss."

Her mouth dropped open. "You bad girl! Here you're making me out to be the common criminal when it's you who's the expert."

"I'm definitely no expert. And technically, I didn't steal them. I watched the tapes from the factory when I found them. Since I own the darn place, I figured they were my property."

Daphne rolled her eyes as I pulled up in front of the Crooked Coffee. Hurrying inside, I was relieved to discover Gabriel wasn't there. I couldn't lie to him again, and I knew he would ask what I was up to. Armed with coffee, I headed back out and ran smack into George Cannon.

"Sorry," I mumbled.

He glared at me. "Watch where you're going."

"I said I was sorry. You could have looked up yourself, you know," I grumbled before heading for the car.

Daphne was staring at me when I got in. "That was close!"

"It isn't like he knows we have the security footage."

"Unless he does. What if he's been watching us? Maybe he followed us to the museum."

I looked out the window and saw him inside the coffee shop, staring back at us. "Let's get out of here. That man is creeping me out!"

By the time we got back to my house, I was a wreck. I kept looking in the rearview mirror expecting to see George following us.

"It's fine," Daphne assured me. "Let's get inside and lock the doors."

I nodded and grabbed the bags from the backseat. I didn't want to risk him pulling up behind me and catching us red-handed with the tapes. It was probably my overactive imagination at play, but I couldn't take any chances.

CHAPTER 8

"Make yourself comfortable," I said, gesturing at the couch.

I had unhooked the VCR a couple months ago and never thought I would need it again. I was getting my ten bucks worth out of the thing, that was for sure.

"I love your house," Daphne commented.

"Thank you, but I really think of it as my grandmother's house. All the furniture is hers. Most of the pictures and décor are hers. I feel like I live here, but it isn't really mine."

She smiled. "It is yours. She wanted you to have it. Enjoy it. It's absolutely beautiful. In time, you'll come to see it as your own and you'll get to pass everything down to your own children."

"Slow down, there turbo. Let's not get ahead of ourselves."

She giggled. "I can already see you and Gabriel living here, happily ever after."

I rolled my eyes. I couldn't think that far ahead. "Okay, got it. Are you ready for this?"

"What do you think we're going to see? It's the

museum. The perps took two things. It isn't like it will be a smash and grab, considering everything in the place is right out in the open, which is still a serious problem if you ask me. How is the place supposed to be taken seriously if they don't even bother trying to pretend the stuff is valuable?"

"A problem for another day," I replied with a shrug. I was getting quite good at letting go of things I didn't need to worry about. I supposed when my more pressing worries involved dark powers being given an injection and the secrets of witches out for all the world to see, well, other concerns didn't seem like a big deal.

I pushed play and waited. There were several seconds of static before an image of four split screens appeared.

"You take the two on the left and I'll take the right," Daphne instructed.

I wrinkled my nose. "Oh wow, these are black and white."

"Are you really that surprised? The cameras are probably older than we are," she joked.

"Look, there's a date stamp," I said pointing to the corner of the screen.

"This is from two weeks ago. We need to find the tapes from the past week."

I shrugged. "What if we see someone casing the place, looking suspicious."

"If we're going to watch these, I want to see something a little more exciting, like actual theft," Daphne countered.

"Fine," I said, shutting off the tape, intending to switch to the tapes from last week.

Both of our phones chimed at the same time. I reached for mine and realized it was a group text to all of us from my mother.

"Uh oh," Daphne said. "That can't be good."

"I'll call her," I said, pushing her name on the phone.

She picked up right away. "Where are you?" she asked a little out of breath.

"I'm at home. What's up?"

"I'm coming right over. Is Daphne with you?"

"Yes."

"Good, we're on our way."

"Who is we, Mom?"

"All of us," she said, and disconnected the call.

I groaned. "They're on their way here."

"What! Do they know what we did? How could they possibly know already? It's been less than an hour!" Daphne said in a panic.

"I don't know, but we better put this stuff away," I said, grabbing the tape out of the VCR and stashing it in the bags. I stowed the bags in one of the kitchen cabinets.

"Did she say why they were coming?" Daphne asked.

"No, but she sounded pretty freaked out. I'm sure it's another crisis. You would think we could get through the first one before we were hit with another."

"Maybe they stole the chest back," she offered.

"I hope so. I want all of this done and over."

It wasn't long before there was a knock on the door. The first to arrive were Magnolia and my mother who were quickly followed by Lila and Coral.

"What's up?" I asked, trying to be casual as I glanced around the living room where they were arrayed.

"We have a problem," my mother said, wringing her hands.

"What happened?" Lila asked.

Magnolia shot her a glare, taking Daphne and I both by surprise.

"Show them," my mother said to Magnolia.

We all waited while Magnolia dug into her purse. When she pulled out two small scraps of paper, I was rather unimpressed.

"What are those?" I asked, hoping my mother wasn't freaking out over nothing.

"Notes."

Lila snatched one of the notes out of Magnolia's hand. I waited. Lila gasped, and I reached for the other note.

It was a plain piece of white paper. The brief message looked to be calligraphy writing scrawled in a deep black ink.

"What is this?" I asked, reading the message out loud. "Naughty, naughty. Magical lock picking."

Daphne made a noise. I turned to look at her, my eyes wide.

"What does Lila's say?" Daphne asked.

Lila waved it in the air. "Oh goodness. That inkwell needs to mind its own business."

I had to laugh. We were talking about an object. Not a human. "Read it out loud," I demanded.

Coral snatched the note and stared at it. "A love spell is in the air."

"Does that mean what I think it means?" Daphne asked, her eyes wide.

My mother was nodding her head. "Yes. This is the work of the inkwell."

"Where did you find these?" I asked.

"I got one in my mailbox and Magnolia got the other," my mother answered.

"What's the one about a lock?" Coral asked.

Daphne and I exchanged a look, knowing we were busted.

"What did you do?" my mom questioned us, looking back and forth between us.

"We snuck into the office at the museum," Daphne said.

I knew she was only telling half the story to protect us, but I had a feeling it was pointless. My mother and her witchy friends were way too keen for that.

"Why would you do that?" Magnolia asked, both hands on her hips. "And you used magic? Didn't we warn you against using magic?" she scolded.

"I did it. It was just a little magic. I didn't think it would be noticeable," I admitted.

"Never mind all of that. We've got to find that inkwell. The notes were put into our boxes this time, but what happens if they are given to the sheriff or that silly supernatural investigator?" Lila said.

"Does the inkwell know who did the casting?" I asked. "I thought you said it didn't know."

"It doesn't," Coral answered.

"Then why would the notes appear in your boxes?" I asked the group in general.

No one seemed to have an answer, which wasn't exactly comforting.

"Everyone have a seat," I said, taking control of the situation. All of the women were clearly distraught. "I'll grab us some water."

I walked into the kitchen, Daphne following on my heels. I pulled open the fridge, grabbing six bottles of water.

"This can't be good," Daphne mumbled.

"We have to tell them about the tapes," I told her.

She scrunched up her nose. "Do we have to? You know they'll only lecture us again."

I shrugged. "I have a feeling they're going to find out anyway. May as well get it out in the open."

"I hate it when you're sensible," she grumbled.

I chuckled. "Me too, but I know my mother and she isn't going to let it go. Besides, if we find out who took the stupid things, they'll have something to do."

We carried the waters back out and passed them around. The room was very somber.

"Why did you girls break into the museum?" Coral asked.

I looked at Daphne, who clearly didn't want me to tell them, but I felt like we had no choice. "We took the security tapes."

"More security tapes?" my mother asked with an eyebrow raised.

Lila started giggling. "What is it with you and security tapes. Did you find our culprit?"

"Not yet. We'd just started watching when you guys showed up," Daphne explained.

"I overheard Harold and George talking at the post office. George admits to having the chest, but he swears he didn't steal it. From what I could glean from the conversation, he says the chest just showed up on his porch," I explained, glad everyone was together so I wouldn't have to repeat the information.

"He stole it. Obviously, he stole it," Coral said with irritation.

"Why hasn't Harold confiscated it?" my mom asked.

We all looked at each other and then to Lila. She was the one who had the man enamored with her. If anyone could find out why, it would be her.

"I'll ask him. Right now, I'm simply trying to keep him away from anything supernatural," she said.

"I think they're in cahoots together," Coral stated.

"It's certainly possible," I added. "Harold has definitely been a little too interested in things since that whole factory business. He's making me nervous, and the two of them did seem a little familiar."

"Which is why I have him under my spell," Lila replied.

"I hope you can keep him reined in. With this other business going on, we don't have time to worry about Harold snooping around," Coral said, irritation evident in her voice.

"I'll do my best," Lila replied with a toss of her hair.

My mom turned their way, casting a disapproving glare

between them. She had always been the peacekeeper, which was probably why she was considered the leader of the coven.

She grabbed Lila's hands in her own. "Thank you, Lila. We all appreciate what you are doing for us. We know you're doing your best."

"Thank you, Lila. I didn't mean to sound as if I didn't appreciate what you were doing," Coral added with a sigh.

"Okay, that's settled. Don't let us keep you, girls," Magnolia said, with a warm smile. "Watch away."

Lila stood and dusted invisible lint from her skirt. "We should go. There's nothing we can do now. Everyone needs to resist the urge to use magic until we track down that inkwell. You two figure out who took the chest. We'll do what we can to find out who's behind the inkwell."

My mother stayed behind. "You girls do what you can, but please don't take such big risks."

"I know, Mom. We were careful," I told her.

"Good. Remember, no one knows those items are charmed. Only a witch can sense the power. As long as there are no other witches running about Lemon Bliss, we have some time," she assured us.

"What about that George guy? Violet said he had all kinds of equipment that was supposed to detect ghosts and traces of magic," Daphne asked.

My mom smiled. "Dear, we have dealt with mediums and so-called psychics and every other type of person who believed they could see ghosts and what not. While there are certainly some people who have the gift, they are not quite so bold. Those instruments are hogwash in my opinion. They use them to excite naïve people who don't understand our world. It really is quite sad."

"Then why were you guys so worried about those two guys when they were snooping around the factory?" I asked, a little surprised to hear her take on things.

She grimaced. "I believe one of them did have a magical background. I'm not sure if it was the man who died or his partner. They got a little too close for comfort. I truly hope this George character is not what he says he is. For now, our best choice is to get the items back and secure them. We'll figure out what to do with our unwelcome visitor once we know more."

"Is it always like this?" I asked her, needing to know what I'd gotten myself into.

"No, dear. I promise it's usually not this dramatic. The girls and I have enjoyed a long run, living a largely peaceful existence. While there have always been rumors, most people are fascinated and like the idea of witches roaming about Lemon Bliss. The problems only started when those two men showed up, which is why I really hope we can bore him to death and he moves onto another place. There are more than enough places with supernatural events to investigate."

"I sure hope he gets bored," I muttered.

My mother was about to walk out when she paused. "Have you been charming the old orchard?" she asked, referring to my grandmother's old lemon tree orchard out back.

I had noticed the lemon trees seemed to be getting greener and perking up, but hadn't thought anything of it. I'd attributed it to nothing more than the time of year.

Shaking my head, I eyed her. "No, why do you ask?"

"Oh, just that I can smell them. I'm guessing they'll bear fruit this year and they haven't since your grandmother passed way." Her gaze took a wistful look. "Maybe you'll be able to start producing her tea again."

"Mom, seriously? One thing at a time. I'm glad the lemon trees might bear fruit, but don't go thinking I plan to reopen the factory. That's more work than I'd know what to do with."

She grinned and turned away. "Take care girls and let us know if you find anything useful on those tapes," she said, before walking out the door.

Daphne and I looked at each other. "Later?" I asked.

"Yes! I'm going home. I'm behind on laundry and my house looks like a tornado hit it. The tapes can wait."

I laughed. "I'll see you tomorrow."

Once Daphne left I took a look around my own house. It wasn't exactly a disaster, but it could use a little tidying up.

CHAPTER 9

The following Monday was off to a good start. We were settling into a rhythm at the bakery and had managed two nights straight without midnight meetings at the factory. Things were looking up except for the minor missing chest and inkwell drama. The threat of the witches being exposed or dark powers being unleashed was hovering in the back of my thoughts, but I did my best to ignore it.

Daphne drifted into the kitchen midday, leaving the door to the front serving area open.

"Slow?" I asked her, rolling out a piecrust.

"Yep. Just finished up with the last group. Did you watch any more of those video tapes yesterday?"

"No. I got busy cleaning up and finally unpacked the last few boxes I had."

"I still have boxes to unpack. I keep thinking if they've been packed this long, maybe I don't need whatever's in them."

"Good point. Maybe take a look and see what's in them before you toss them out. You never know."

The bells on the front door tinkled, and Daphne turned to see who it was. "Hi, Lila," she greeted.

From the front of the counter I could hear Lila's voice. "Is Violet back there?"

"I'm here, Lila. Let me slide this pie in the oven, and I'll be right out," I called.

Daphne let the door close behind her as she stepped back out front. I steeled myself before I joined her. There was always the chance Lila stopped by to give us more concerning news. I hadn't used a bit of magic. It wasn't me that was in trouble this time. At least, I could be confident of that.

After washing my hands, I headed out front, my little timer in my hand so I wouldn't forget about the pies in the oven. Lila and Daphne were sitting at a table chatting away.

"I love the new color, Lila," I said, smiling as I took in her rather vivid violet hair color.

She fluffed it lightly and smiled. "Harold said he loved my purple hair. I figured I'd give him what he really likes."

I nodded and sat down. "What brings you by?" I asked, hoping it wasn't more bad news.

"I'm meeting Harold here. He's been dying to come by and try some of your cookies. I'm doing everything I can to keep the man occupied. He still hasn't said anything about that darn chest," she grumbled.

As if on cue, Harold pulled open the front door. Lila smiled brightly and waved to Harold.

"Lila! I've missed you so much!" he exclaimed, walking towards her.

"Good morning, Harold," I greeted.

He barely noticed I was there. He only had eyes for Lila.

"How's it going, Sheriff Smith," Daphne said, as if testing his attention span.

Harold wouldn't look away from Lila. Wow, her love

spell appeared to have worked, like *magic*. He was absolutely enthralled with her.

"Can we get you anything?" I asked Lila, figuring Harold wouldn't answer me.

She smiled. "I'm going to visit the ladies room. I'll grab something when I get back," she said and stood up from where she was seated at a table.

Harold jumped up and looked as if he would follow her into the bathroom. Lila cast a smile his way. "You wait right here." He did as he was told, but it was clear he wasn't happy about it.

Glancing to Harold, I asked, "Would you like a cookie?"

He finally looked my way. "Oh yes. Chocolate chip if you have it."

Rounding the counter, I grabbed a cookie for him and carried it over.

"So has there been any more news about that break-in at the museum?" I asked, hoping to get some information out of him.

He seemed to be more himself when Lila wasn't directly in front of him. He took a bite of the cookie and sighed. "Delicious!"

"Thank you. Any word on that break in?" I asked, steering him back to the topic at hand.

"Nope," he replied.

It annoyed me to no end he was lying straight to my face. I had to bite my tongue to keep from spilling that I'd overheard him talking to George about the chest.

"Oh, really, I thought I heard a rumor someone had found one of the items," I said, hoping to nudge him. Maybe the love spell left him a little cloudy.

Harold shrugged a shoulder. "Oh, I hear rumors all the time. Some people like to think they are more involved than they truly are. I have to weed those folks out."

"What do you mean?" I asked.

He looked at me, suspicion entering his gaze. "I mean, you can't always believe everything you hear or *overhear.*"

I gulped. Did he know I'd been eavesdropping that day at the post office? Did that mean he was protecting George, or was he implying he didn't believe George actually had the chest? The way he was staring at me made me feel like he knew something I didn't. Maybe he had dark powers and we didn't know it. What if he had opened the chest?

"Do you know who did it?" Daphne asked, getting right to the point

He shrugged a shoulder. "That supernatural guy, he's definitely a suspect, but I have no concrete evidence. It's still early in the investigation."

I rolled my eyes. It was a line. I knew it was something they probably trained police to say. It was a *cop out* in the truest sense of the word.

"Oh," I murmured, biting my tongue so I didn't say anything to offend the man.

Harold returned his attention to his cookie. I was just glad to have his focus on something other than me. I made a mental note to ask my mother more about the missing chest. I needed to know if the person who opened the chest absorbed the powers, or if they floated around the universe. Sweet tea, these days the things I worried about were just crazy.

"I heard it was some teenagers," I offered, hoping to get Harold to keep chatting.

I knew the moment Lila returned, he would lose the ability to think straight. Her spell was a little too effective. I doubted he would be able to tell Lila anything but how much he loved her.

He chewed and nodded his head. "I have a couple suspects in mind."

"Who?" Daphne and I asked in unison.

"There's a young woman that has shown up on my radar,

Darlene Clayton. Another lady, Rosa Herrera. I don't know her all that well. Her name came up when I was doing some digging, too," he offered.

"How..." I started to ask.

Lila came out of the bathroom at that moment, and it was as if a switch was flipped. Harold's focus narrowed to her, his eyes tracking her every step as she walked across the bakery.

"Oh, that looks good," Lila said with a smile, eyeing the last bite or so of the cookie.

"Here, you can have it, my love," Harold said, holding it out.

"I'll get you one, Lila," I said, getting up from the table.

She smiled and patted Harold's hand. "You finish it, dear. I have to watch my figure," she winked.

"You're perfect just the way you are," he assured her.

Gag me. The man was absolutely gaga for her. I felt a little guilty, but I had a feeling Lila was actually fond of him and didn't mind the attention at all.

I fetched a cookie for Lila and waited by their table, hoping to get a little more information from Harold. I had no idea the man actually had suspects. I didn't recognize either name.

"Sheriff, what makes you believe Rosa or Darlene had anything to do with the theft at the museum?"

Lila raised an eyebrow in question. All three of us women stared at Harold, hoping he would give us a clue, but he didn't appear to have heard me.

"Are they locals?" Daphne asked. "Do we know them?"

Harold simply smiled at Lilia, oblivious to our presence in general. I looked at Lila, begging her with my eyes to get the man to speak.

She grabbed his hand. "Harold, the girls are asking you questions about a young lady named Rosa."

"And Darlene," I added quickly.

"You're so beautiful," he mumbled, staring into Lila's eyes.

It was a lost cause.

"Okay, well, I better get back to work," I mumbled, realizing we weren't going to get anywhere with Lila around.

"Harold, go on out to the car, and I'll be there in a minute," she instructed him.

"I'll miss you," he offered as he stood from the table. At her wave, he walked out of the bakery.

When he was out the door I turned to Lila, hands on my hips. "How are we ever going to get anything out of him when he can't think of anything besides you?"

"The spell was a little more effective than I anticipated. I'll ask him about those names. Who are they?"

I shrugged a shoulder. "I have no idea. He said they were suspects, but I didn't get a chance to ask him why before you came out of the bathroom. I'm not sure that spell was such a good idea."

"It's keeping him occupied though, that's for sure," Daphne said with a chuckle.

Lila nodded. "Yes, it is, and that was the whole point. I'll see what I can find out. You girls find out who those women are. We all have our jobs to do and mine is keeping that man out of our business."

I rolled my eyes, "I can see what a difficult job that is."

Lila grinned and smoothed back her purple hair. "Someone has to do it."

Once she left, I turned to Daphne. "Have you ever heard those names before?"

She shook her head. "I don't think so, but I haven't been back in Lemon Bliss that long either."

"So, do you think Lila is enjoying that spell a little too much?" I asked.

Daphne rolled her eyes and shook her head. "How is that not personal gain? Lila has always had a little crush on

Harold. Now, she's taking one for the team," she said, creating air quotes with her fingers.

"Yep, I just hope that spell doesn't backfire on us."

We didn't get a chance to talk further. A cluster of customers came through the door. I checked the timer in my pocket and headed for the kitchen to check my pies and move onto the next project.

As I worked, I wracked my brain, trying to place the names with faces. I knew most people in town, but there were a few new faces I wasn't familiar with. Gabriel might know. I checked my watch and hoped I'd see him soon. We had barely spoken yesterday, but he did promise to stop by sometime today.

It would give me a few minutes to pick his brain. That wasn't the only reason. If I involved him in this one piece of the puzzle, he would hopefully forgive me for being so cagey the other day.

CHAPTER 10

*W*e were in the midst of the afternoon lull, which meant I could stay in the kitchen. I turned on my playlist and let myself unwind as I baked. I was just finishing up another batch of chocolate chip cookies, which tended to sell the best to the after-school crowd, when I heard the bells up front.

"Violet!" Daphne called out.

"Coming," I said, quickly washing my hands and pulling off my apron.

I walked out front to find Gabriel there with coffee and a bouquet of flowers. My heart did a little flip as I met his blue eyes. I had to find a way to share some of my secrets with him. I didn't care what my mom and the others thought. I trusted him, and they could too. I would protect him should anything bad happen.

I hoped.

"Hi," I said, taking the flowers.

We walked to one of the empty tables and sat down. Daphne was grinning ear to ear, but turned away to wait on some customers.

"I'm sorry," he blurted out. "I know there are things you can't tell me, and I'm okay with it. I mean, I don't like it all the time, but I guess if I want to be with you, I have to expect you'll have some secrets."

I sighed. "I'm sorry too. I knew you were upset and wasn't sure how to deal with it. All this witch stuff is, well, I'm still figuring everything out. Apparently, there are some things I'm not supposed to talk about. No matter what, I don't want you to think I make a habit of keeping secrets," I explained.

He held up a hand. "It's fine. I get it."

"Thank you," I whispered.

"How's it been going here today?" he asked, quickly changing the subject.

"Not bad," I said, pausing to take a sip of the coffee he'd brought me. "Harold stopped by. That was interesting."

"Oh, yeah?"

I quickly filled him in on what I had overheard at the post office and filled him in on Harold's suspects. I left out the specific details about the chest.

"Do you know either of them?" I asked, hoping he would have some insight.

"I know of Rosa. I haven't really talked with her. She's been here since I moved here a couple years ago. I don't know that I've really seen her around town all that much now that I think about it. Maybe she works in Ruby Red or something."

"What about the other one, Darlene?"

He looked thoughtful for a minute. "She's relatively new. I mean, I know she was here before you, but I couldn't really say exactly when she showed up. She's another one that I know of, but haven't really seen around much."

"I wonder why Harold suspects them?" I mused aloud.

"I don't know. I do remember one time I ran into Rosa at the post office. She's not the friendliest sort. I bumped into her and apologized. You'd have thought I hauled off and hit her with the look she gave me."

"Hmm, that's odd. I can't believe I've never seen either one of them."

"You probably have, but never paid attention."

I sighed. I wished Gabriel knew more, but it was what it was. I would have to do my own snooping around. "I guess I know what I have to do."

"Please be careful. If either of those women are truly suspects, it's for good reason. You never know what they may be capable of," he warned.

"I will."

"I've got to get going. I'll give you a call tonight. Maybe I can bring dinner over?" he asked, hopefully.

"I actually have plans tonight," I said, with a grin.

"Oh, really? You have another boyfriend I should know about?" he joked.

I winked. "Yep, she's right over there. Daphne and I have a girl's night planned. We are going to eat pizza and drink a bottle of wine to celebrate our first week of successful business."

He flashed a grin. "Tomorrow then?"

"Sounds perfect."

I gave him a quick kiss goodbye and sent him on his way.

Daphne was standing at the counter, grinning like a fool. "He really likes you. I hope you tell our mothers to get over it. Gabriel isn't going anywhere, and you didn't even have to cast some hokey spell."

"I think I'm going to have another talk with the ladies. I'm okay with being in the coven, but I'm not going to let it dictate my life. I'm not going to do anything rash, but the subject is definitely not closed. I don't like keeping secrets."

"Good. I'll back you up," she vowed.

I headed back into the kitchen and got right to work. I

hadn't gotten much done before my mother stopped by and requested I sit down and chat with her. I was beginning to dread these conversations. Each time she stopped by unannounced, it was to deliver more bad news or heap more stress on my plate. I missed the days we could laugh and simply talk about normal things.

"We're slow," Daphne said, "Take a break. Relax."

I grabbed a bottle of water and took one for my mom before joining her at a table. "What's up?" I asked, dreading what she was going to say.

"Oh, nothing serious. I've just been a little lost today."

I could see the melancholy on her face. "Mom, are you sure you're okay?"

She offered a wan smile. "I'm just so worried about our future. You just got back to town and we haven't even had a chance to really enjoy each other. I had such grand plans to show you the way of things and now here we are facing another crisis."

I reached across the table and squeezed her hand. "It's okay. Really. I'm sure all of this is going to be fine."

"That chest," she said, shaking her head. "If someone manages to open it, we're in for real trouble. I'm terrified, Violet. I truly am. It isn't only us at risk either, but witches everywhere. Innocent lives could be ruined should that evil be allowed to run unchecked."

"Do you know exactly what's in the chest?" I asked.

She shook her head. "Not really. The information has been passed down from one generation to the next, but you know how things can get lost in translation."

"Then maybe it isn't as bad as you think," I offered.

She smirked. "Oh, honey. I learned a long time ago that it's always as bad as I think. That's my gift. I know when doom is looming, and I can guarantee you, it's out there, waiting to strike."

"Mom, you don't have to be so gloom and doom. Haven't

we had this same discussion before?" I teased, thinking back to the whole business with the dead man in the factory.

That had been a big fuss and, when all was said and done, it was an accident. A tragic accident, but an accident nonetheless.

"Oh hon, if that nosy man, George Cannon, has that chest, I'm afraid doomsday may be putting it mildly."

I shrugged a shoulder, still not interested in freaking out and getting worked up over something that hadn't even happened yet. Mind you, in the middle of the night, my mind ran in circles over these worries, but I was doing my best not to let that be the case all day every day. "I thought you said only a witch would know what to do with the chest or recognize what was inside?"

"That's true."

"Then we don't have to worry about George opening it, right?"

She shook her head. "Anyone who knows how to use magic could summon the necessary powers to open it."

"I don't think the man is inherently evil. I think he's curious and a bit of a busy body who's seeking attention, but I don't think he's about to summon evil spirits," I told her with completely honesty.

She smiled, and it was a real smile. "How did you get so smart?"

I giggled. "I had a good teacher."

"Okay, I'll try not to worry too much, but Violet, this is very serious. Even if he can't open it and release the evil, I'm sure he could find a way to expose our secrets. That stupid inkwell may very well do that for us," she said with a sigh.

"We know George has the chest. He's had it for days and hasn't done anything. I think we have time to figure it out. If he's innocent of the theft, he isn't our problem. If someone else put that chest on his porch, they did it on purpose, hoping he would eventually figure it out," I reasoned, hoping I was right.

She nodded and took a long drink of water. "I hope you're right."

"Daphne and I will watch the security videos tonight. Harold did mention a couple of names. I'll do some checking to see what I can find out."

"Thank you, Violet. You are always so levelheaded. I'm going to go to the factory and check our book. Maybe there's something in there about that inkwell. If we could freely use magic, this whole situation could be resolved."

"Or it could make it worse. Let's do it the old-fashioned way first, then we panic," I grinned.

"On a much easier topic to discuss, how's business today?" she asked.

"A little slower, which is actually kind of nice. We've still been busy, but it's leveling off. I should get back to the kitchen, so I can wrap things up and get out of here at a decent hour," I told her, standing up from my chair.

"I won't keep you. Do call if you see anything interesting on those tapes."

"I will. Bye mom," I said, giving her a quick hug before she left.

Moments later, Daphne walked into the kitchen, shaking her head. "Those women are going to give themselves ulcers."

I laughed. "You're right. Hopefully we can find something on those tapes tonight."

She looked at the clock on the wall. "A couple more hours and then it's wine time!"

"You can't get sloshed. Remember we're supposed to be running an investigation."

She grinned. "I can get buzzed and you can be the serious one—as usual."

"Not fair!"

She laughed and walked back up front. The bell over the door jingled and voices drifted back to me.

I got busy rolling out piecrusts and thought about everything we knew thus far. I was very curious about Rosa and Darlene, Harold's mysterious suspects.

CHAPTER 11

*S*hortly before closing time, I finished cleaning up the kitchen and meandered out front to find Daphne sitting on a stool behind the register, flipping through a magazine.

"This is kind of a nice change, huh?"

She smiled and nodded, looking a little guilty. "Yes, and I'm taking full advantage of it. Look at this," she said holding up the magazine. It was then I realized she had a restaurant supply catalog. That could be dangerous in Daphne's hands.

"What's that?"

"A fancy coffee machine. We've got to up our game in the coffee world. I don't think we'll be competition for Crooked Coffee, but it is a great way to increase profits without really adding much work," she explained.

I would be thrilled to have a coffee machine in the place. It would make my life so much easier. "Let's do it!"

"Really? I can order this?"

"Definitely. Make sure you get all the supplies as well," I added.

She jumped off her stool and grabbed a small notebook.

"While you're doing that, I'll be in the kitchen doing some research on those two women Harold mentioned."

She was busy jotting down stuff in her little book. "Okay, sounds good," she mumbled.

Returning to the kitchen, I pulled out my laptop and took a seat on a stool by the counter. Typing Darlene's name into the search bar, I waited.

It took a bit to filter through the names until I found a few of her social media profiles. That gave me an idea of where she lived before, and from there, I narrowed my search.

"Wow," I whispered into the room. Darlene was a city girl. She had spent a great deal of time in New York City. How in the world had she ended up in Lemon Bliss, Louisiana? The town didn't even show up on most maps.

I clicked on a link to an archived newspaper article, which led me down a rabbit hole.

"Daphne!" I called out.

She pushed open the kitchen door. "What's wrong?" she asked.

"Look!" I said, showing her my laptop.

She quickly read the article. "Oh my! Is that *the* Darlene?"

I nodded my head. "As far as I can tell. Do you recognize her?"

She studied the picture. "I don't know. She looks familiar, but I can't place her."

"Do you see what it says?" I asked excitedly. "She has to be the one who stole from the museum. It's a pattern!"

Daphne didn't look convinced. "That article says she was stealing artifacts and making forgeries. She made money on that scheme. She isn't going to make any money on an old chest that holds no real value. And, she didn't replace it with a different one. It doesn't seem like her M.O."

I burst out laughing. "You have watched too many movies. Her M.O.?" I asked.

She laughed. "You know what I mean. Doesn't it seem kind of far-fetched?"

I shrugged. "I'm not all that familiar with the minds of criminals."

Daphne stared at the woman's image. "I know her from somewhere."

"Maybe we'll see her on the videos tonight! If we can prove she did it, then we can take the chest back from George. We'll tell him we know he's innocent and maybe he'll be so grateful to us for proving his innocence, he'll back off of the supernatural investigation," I said, my mind whirring as I thought of all of this being wrapped up neat and tidy by tomorrow morning.

Daphne looked at me, one brow raised. "Now who's the one who's watched too many movies?"

"Come on. You have to admit it's a strange coincidence between the two situations. Those things have been in that museum for decades and no one has touched them. Most people aren't even interested in them and only see them as something from the old days. Then, this Darlene woman shows up in town and they suddenly go missing."

"We don't know how long she's been here. We know it's been at least six months, probably longer. Why would she wait until now to take the items?" Daphne asked.

She had a point, but I wasn't ready to give up on my theory. "What if she had been casing the place, waiting for the right time."

Daphne rolled her eyes. "You saw how easy it was for us to break into the place. I don't think she would have had to wait months to grab what she wanted."

"Maybe she did. Maybe she did some research and discovered what the chest and inkwell really were," I said in a low voice. The thought of her knowing the magical qualities of each was a little scary. "Maybe, she's working with George! That has to be it!"

Now I had Daphne's attention. She cocked her head to the side. "I don't know. I guess you could be right. We need to watch those tapes."

I looked up at the clock. "Ten minutes. Let's make sure we're ready for closing, so we can leave on time," I told her, determined more than ever to prove my theory.

"For your sake, I hope you're right. I think I prefer it to be the investigator guy. I don't like the idea of an enemy living among us for months without any of us being the wiser. That doesn't say much for our super senses, does it?"

"No, but maybe she's cloaked somehow. I mean, if the enchantments in the chest were designed to protect witches from detection, maybe she's a bad witch and falls under the same protection."

Daphne threw her hands up in surrender. "You're making my head spin. Relax, put that away and let's take this one step at a time. You're going to drive yourself crazy as well as me."

I sighed, knowing she was right. I did tend to jump to conclusions. Darlene may be completely innocent. I wouldn't pull out the pitchfork just yet. I would wait until I had some kind of concrete proof.

"Fine," I muttered, but if I see her on that security footage..." I left the threat hanging. Truly, I didn't know exactly what I would do. I'd figure it out when the time came.

The bells on the front door jingled, alerting us to a customer. Daphne walked out front. After she said hello, I recognized Harold's voice drifting back to me.

"Perfect," I said to myself, closing my laptop. I wanted to find out how much he really knew about this Darlene woman. If he knew her past, it would explain why she was one of his suspects.

"Hi, Harold," I said walking out front, glad to see he was alone.

Lila would have made it difficult for him to think straight. I wanted his full attention.

"Hello, Miss Broussard," he said with a wide smile.

I inwardly groaned. Clearly, he was still feeling the effects of Lila's spell.

"I was just thinking about you," I said, hoping to charm him.

"Really?" he asked, sounding surprised.

"Yes, I was wondering if you had any more ideas about the theft at the museum? I did some digging on one of the women you mentioned," I said, hoping to get him talking.

Daphne handed him his chocolate chip cookie. *Good.* The way to the man's brain was through his belly.

I followed him to a table and sat down with him. "Lila's meeting me here," he said, still smiling.

"Oh, that's nice."

He nodded and took a bite of his cookie. "It certainly is. Isn't she the most beautiful woman you've ever seen?"

I bit my tongue to keep from giggling. "Harold, about that woman, Darlene. I did some digging into her background. Do you know who she is?"

He shrugged a shoulder. "I'm not worried about Darlene. I'm focusing on that George character."

"You are?" I asked in surprise. "I thought you said you were convinced it wasn't him?"

"I said it was an ongoing investigation. That means I'm investigating leads. I go where the evidence leads me."

"Oh, I see. Have you looked into Darlene's background?" I pressed.

Yesterday I had been convinced it was George, but after what I read online, I was more inclined to believe George and suspect Darlene.

"I know a bit. Why? What makes you think she did it?" he asked in between bites.

"I read an article about her past in New York City. She was accused of stealing various artifacts from a museum and replacing them with forgeries," I explained. "Maybe that's what she did here."

He nodded sagely. "Yep, I know all about that, but she was never actually convicted. There was no evidence. People can speculate all they want, but if there's no proof, you can't do much about it."

"But doesn't that at least warrant you looking a little closer at her and her whereabouts?"

He raised an eyebrow. "Are you trying to tell me how to do my job?"

"Oh no, not at all," I said, realizing I didn't want to push too far.

"I'm looking into all possible leads. I don't think she did it. Nothing was put in place of the stolen items," he pointed out.

"I know, but maybe that's because she didn't think anybody would miss them," I reasoned.

He took another bite. While he chewed, I tried to think of a better way to say what I thought he should do. I didn't have to bother.

Lila breezed through the door and Harold transformed from cop to mush. That silly love spell was making things difficult.

"Hi, Lila," I said tersely.

She looked at me, her brows hitching up. "Something wrong, dear?"

"Not at all. I was just talking to Harold about the museum investigation. I did some digging and found some information I thought was pertinent to the case."

Harold had practically forgotten I was there and waved for Lila to take my seat. "Sit, sit, my dear," he told Lila.

I stood, vacating my chair. Daphne was at the counter, a gleam in her eyes when I glanced her way. She shrugged one shoulder as if to say there was nothing to be done about it.

She was right. There was nothing we could do as long as Harold was mooning over Lila. He wasn't looking into us, but he wasn't looking into the museum business either. I couldn't stand to watch the scene in our dining area and headed back into the kitchen. I had to trust Lila knew what she was doing.

CHAPTER 12

*N*ot much later after we'd practically booted Harold out of the bakery and I'd made it home, I changed into a pair of stretchy pants and pulled on a long t-shirt before heading downstairs. Daphne would be over any minute. I was looking forward to finally reviewing the security tapes from the museum.

Pausing by the kitchen window, I looked out. It was dusk, the sun low on the horizon, the old lemon tree orchard cast in shadow against the sky behind it. The scent of lemons drifted through the windows. I loved that smell. It was reminiscent of my grandmother. Back when she still had the factory open, she'd fuss over the orchards, often walking amongst the trees. I now knew she was likely charming them. I wondered what had helped the trees along this year because it certainly wasn't me.

The doorbell rang, breaking into my brief reverie. I hurried over to open the front door. Daphne stood there holding a pizza box and a bottle of wine.

"Are you ready to get this party started?" she asked with a grin.

"I am. I've got cheese and crackers laid out as well and a bottle of red wine."

She walked in and slid the pizza box on the coffee table. "I almost ate a piece on the way over here. It smelled so good and I'm starving. I don't think I could eat another cookie or muffin, which reminds me, I need to pack a healthy lunch tomorrow. I'm going to gain twenty pounds this month alone if I keep snacking on your delicious treats coming out of that kitchen."

I laughed. "Trust me, I went through the same thing the first year or so when I started out. You'll become immune to the smells and the temptation."

"I hope so."

"I'll grab a couple of glasses," I said, walking towards the kitchen.

Returning, I delivered the wineglasses, paper plates and a stack of napkins to the coffee table in front of the couch.

"Cue up the movie. I'm almost afraid I am going to be bored and fall asleep," Daphne mumbled between bites of pizza.

"I hope not. I'm putting way too much hope in the idea we are going to find something. If we don't, it'll be a bummer."

After starting the tape, I settled onto the couch beside her. We watched in silence for several minutes, both of us enjoying pizza and drinking wine. It would have been a fun, relaxing evening if there wasn't so much riding on us finding something to bring the whole situation to an end.

"That was a waste of time," Daphne said when the first tape came to an end and we saw nothing but groups of tourists meandering through the museum.

I put in the next tape and flopped back on the couch, quickly losing hope we would find anything.

"There!" Daphne jumped up and shouted.

I stood as well, getting close to the TV to see the image a

little better. "That's her! That's her!" I clapped with glee. "That's Darlene!"

"Wait, let's see if we can see if she takes anything," Daphne cautioned.

Unfortunately, there wasn't any real action. Darlene was spotted walking around the museum, but she certainly didn't take anything that we could see.

"This is the day the chest was taken," I said, pointing to the date stamp. "She just looked directly at the camera! She knows she's being recorded."

In my mind, that made her guilty. Why would she go to the museum, scout it out and then look at the camera? She was obviously trying to determine where the cameras were aimed.

"Why didn't we start with this one?" she asked.

I shrugged. "The tapes aren't marked. I didn't think of it," I said, embarrassed I had overlooked such an obvious detail.

"She isn't doing anything," Daphne pointed out. "Look! She's leaving!"

I paused the tape, looking to see if there was anything in her hands. They were empty.

"Maybe she'll come back later," I said hopefully.

We settled back on the couch, sipping our wine while intently staring at the television.

"Who's that?" I asked.

"I don't know everyone in Lemon Bliss," Daphne countered.

"No, look. That woman is walking with a cane. Gabriel told me Harold's other suspect, Rosa, had a cane."

"Violet, a lot of people use canes," she said dryly.

I watched as the woman walked to the small table where the chest was on display. She read the small plaque in front of it.

"She's not moving," I whispered.

Daphne leaned forward on the couch, her gaze focused

on the image. "Take it," she breathed out. "We got you. Take it."

She didn't take it. Instead, Rosa moved on and inspected many of the items on display before pausing in front of the inkwell.

"This has to be it," I said, hoping we had finally found our culprit.

We watched as the woman walked back to the chest. She reached out a hand to touch it, but quickly yanked it back as if she had been burned.

"What was that?" Daphne asked, looking at me with wide eyes.

I shook my head. "I have no idea, but we definitely need to tell the others about this."

I was convinced she was our culprit but when she walked out the door empty handed, I was ready to give up.

"This feels…"

"That's him!" I shouted at the TV.

Daphne leaned forward with me as we watched intently. George Cannon had just walked past Rosa into the museum. They exchanged a look before he proceeded directly to the chest. We could see Rosa at the front door watching him. When he noticed her, she spun around and left.

"That was odd," I mumbled.

"I think they know each other. What if they worked together on this heist?" Daphne suggested.

"I think you may be right. It certainly seemed like they knew each other. Maybe all three of them are working together. Darlene and Rosa scouted the place out and discovered where the items were and where the cameras were positioned and now George is moving in to take them."

Daphne was nodding her head. "Look at that big trench

coat he's wearing. Who wears a trench coat when it's still warm out?"

"Good point. What's he doing now?" I asked, squinting to see better, not that it helped.

"It looks like a notebook. He's writing something down," Daphne pointed to the book.

I watched as he studied the chest and then made notes. "Curiouser and curiouser," I said under my breath.

Daphne laughed. "I haven't heard that in a while, but you nailed it. This is all very curious."

George tucked the notebook in his pocket and browsed the museum. When he reached the table with the inkwell, he pulled the notebook out again and started writing.

"Okay, I think it's safe to say he knows those two things are more than just simple artifacts from Lemon Bliss's history," I announced.

"I think you're right, which is *not* good at all. If he knows, that means he may know how to open the chest. Our mothers are going to freak out," she said, shaking her head. "I need more wine to get through this."

I groaned, knowing we had to tell them, but dreading their response. "You know they're going to order an emergency coven meeting."

She nodded. "Yep."

We watched the rest of the tape, but never did see anyone actually take the chest and inkwell.

"How strange is that. They're still there," Daphne said.

"Let's watch the next tape. Maybe they didn't go missing until the following day. That lady running the place could have been mistaken," I reasoned.

Daphne refilled our wine glasses while I switched out the tapes. It took several tries before I found the right day.

"They really need to start labeling these," I complained.

Daphne burst into laughter. "That way when we break

into their office and steal them again, we'll know which tapes we need?"

I rolled my eyes and shrugged. "Yes, exactly. A little courtesy wouldn't go unnoticed," I said in a haughty tone.

We both started giggling. The wine was going straight to our heads.

"They're gone," Daphne said, pointing to the place the chest should have been sitting.

"How is that even possible?" I asked in astonishment.

Daphne shrugged. "They must have disabled the camera before they took the chest. It explains why the two ladies looked at the camera."

"Harold was right to suspect Rosa and Darlene. Now, we have to get him to focus on them as well as George. I think it's plain to see they had something to do with the theft," I said, completely convinced.

"Are you going to call your mother, or am I?" Daphne muttered, leaning her head against the back of the couch.

Glancing her way, I took another swallow of wine and shrugged. "Go for it."

"Ugh," she moaned, reaching for her phone on the coffee table.

I nibbled on another slice of pizza as I listened to Daphne fill her mother in.

"Then one of you will have to pick us up," she said in response to something her mother said. "Neither one of us is legal to drive."

Tapping her screen to end the call, she took a sip of wine before rolling her head to look at me. "Guess what?" she said with a sarcastic smile.

"Hmm, gee, I wonder what it could be."

"Yep, drink up, lady, because my mom is coming to pick us up and take us to the factory for an emergency meeting."

"I'm taking the wine," I said, quickly downing the glass I held in my hand.

Daphne downed her glass too before quickly eating another piece of pizza.

"Can't we talk here?" I asked.

She shook her head. "Nope. They think someone is watching them. They don't want to be seen all together."

I nodded, understanding dawning. "Of course."

It wasn't long before Magnolia showed up to whisk us away to the factory. There was a minor argument over whether or not the bottle of wine was going with us, but Daphne held her ground. We got to the factory before anyone else.

"You girls should be sober for this," Magnolia lectured.

I scoffed. "We're just a little tipsy. If we're facing exposure and dark powers unleashed, I think drunk is the way to be."

Magnolia glared at me, while Daphne laughed.

"Wait until your mother sees what condition you're in," Magnolia said, narrowing her eyes and clucking.

I raised an eyebrow. "My mother knows I'm a big girl. I've been drinking wine a long time. If she hasn't figured that out by now, it's probably best we get it all out on the table," I said, doing my best to keep my speech smooth.

It wasn't long before my mother arrived.

"They're drunk!" Magnolia announced as my mother descended the stairs.

"Tattle tale," I murmured.

Daphne started giggling uncontrollably.

My mother looked at me, sighed and shrugged her shoulders. "They're adults, Magnolia. You drove them, right?"

Magnolia rolled her eyes, but nodded her head in affirmation.

"Drink lots of water and pop some of those vitamins I left at your house," my mother said, before taking her seat on one of the overstuffed couches.

Once everyone arrived and sat down, Daphne and I filled them in on what we saw. The information wasn't exactly groundbreaking, but it did give us a better idea of who to focus on. It was decided the cameras had to have been disabled manually or magically to conceal the evidence, which left more questions than answers.

Everyone was concerned there was another witch in town. Whoever it was, we were concerned they intended to stir up trouble.

CHAPTER 13

*I*t had been two days since our last late night coven meeting. No new news had come forth since then. Lila was supposed to be trying to talk with Harold. My mom and Coral were doing their own investigating to find out more about Darlene and Rosa, while Magnolia tried to warm up to George. I was taking no news as good news for now.

I found myself humming as I scooped cookie dough onto a baking tray. I liked this peaceful existence. I wasn't foolish enough to believe it would last, but I was going to appreciate every minute of it while it did.

The bells on the door jingled and a prickle ran up my spine. I had a sense the peace I had just been enjoying was about to evaporate.

"Violet!" Daphne called from the front.

When I pushed open the kitchen door, I was relieved to see it wasn't a line of customers that had her hollering for me. It was Gabriel. I hadn't seen him in a couple of days while he did a job in New Orleans.

"Hi! You're back!" I said, rounding the counter.

"Did you miss me?" he asked, pausing to drop a kiss on my cheek.

"Of course. How was it?" I asked.

"Good. It was nice to catch up with some old friends, but I'm glad to be back. The city is a little too loud for me. I'd hadn't realized how noisy it was until I lived here," he said, a smile stretching across his face.

He, of course, brought me a coffee. Gesturing toward a table, he followed me over and sat down across from me.

"Next week you can come by and drink a coffee from here," I told him with a smile.

"Really?"

"Yep, Daphne ordered some fancy coffee maker and all the works a couple of days ago. She's excited."

"How's everything else been going?"

I didn't have to ask what he was talking about. He was referring to the missing artifacts.

"It's a mess, as usual."

I quickly gave him the rundown. He nodded along as he listened.

"Wow," he said when I was done.

"I'm going to confront George," I announced, surprising myself. I hadn't realized I was considering it until just then. I was tired of the waiting and wondering. Sometimes, you just had to face something head on instead of skirting around it.

"That's not a good idea," Gabriel replied quickly.

"What do you mean? We have to find out what he wants."

"What if he's dangerous?" he said, his eyes narrowing with concern.

I waved a hand. "I think we would have known that by now. I'm not worried. I'm tired of looking over my shoulder all the time, though."

"Violet, you can't just go knock on the guy's door and demand answers. That's the sheriff's job!" he exclaimed.

"Uh, the sheriff isn't doing his job, so I need to do it for him," I shot back.

Gabriel practically growled under his breath. "It's a bad idea. I don't like it."

I lifted one shoulder. "You don't have to. I'm still doing it."

"Violet, quit being stubborn."

"I'm not being stubborn. If I don't do this, who will?"

He took a sip of his coffee and glanced out the window. I looked over to see Daphne pretending to be busy, but I knew she was listening. A woman was at the counter, also studiously looking away.

I took several deep breaths. "I'm sorry. I'm not trying to be difficult, but trust me, I sense no danger there."

"Let me go with you," he said, looking directly into my eyes.

"What?"

"I want to go with you. You get your way, and I get the satisfaction of being nearby should the guy get any ideas."

"Fine. How about after I close up today?"

He nodded. "I'm not working today. I'll pick you up at your house."

"Sounds good."

He stood, clearly ready to go. "Okay, I'll be by later." At that, he strode out of the bakery. I sensed he had more to say, but was keeping it to himself.

The customer who'd been at the counter slipped into a chair, so I stood and went behind the counter with Daphne.

"Dang, that was intense," she commented.

"Yeah, it was."

"What was that all about?"

I told her my plan to confront George. She basically had the same response Gabriel had. Despite her worry about what could happen, she agreed it was time to face the situation head on and just get it over with.

"But I'm glad Gabriel's going with you. I don't think it's smart to confront George without back up." A sound from outside drew her attention away. "Uh-oh."

"What?"

She used her head to gesture towards the door. "Mom's here and she doesn't look happy."

I turned around to see Magnolia yank the door open, clearly upset about something. I glanced over, mindful of the customers, and asked her to go into the kitchen. I had a feeling she had witch business to discuss, and I didn't want anyone overhearing.

The three of us went into the kitchen with Daphne staying near the door in case another customer came in.

"What's wrong?" I asked.

"There's been another note," Magnolia said in a strained voice.

I immediately held up my hands. "It wasn't me."

"Me either," Daphne echoed.

Magnolia shook her head. "I know. It's about the love spell. Lila's love spell."

"Again?" I asked.

She nodded. "This time the note was in my box. It's as if the inkwell is reminding us it's still out there."

"Is that normal?" Daphne asked.

Magnolia smiled. "I truly don't know, but it concerns me."

"As long as we give it nothing new to write about, it should be okay," I offered.

I didn't tell her I planned on going to George's house. If I could get that inkwell and chest, this would all be over. If I told her, she would only lecture me and warn me about exposing myself. The way I saw it, this little game with a stupid inkwell was far riskier. I was determined to bring it all to an end.

"Don't worry about it, Mom," Daphne said. "It's just a note."

"You don't understand. The note wasn't quite as simple as the first. This time, it accused the caster of the spell of manipulation that would be exposed. It also included what can only be taken as a threat about revealing past spells of a similar nature," she explained.

"What? How? You mean this thing is planning on unveiling every spell ever done in this area? That's going to be a lot of ink," I quipped. "Maybe the well will run dry before it ever happens."

Daphne bit back a chuckle as Magnolia leveled a gaze at me. "I don't think it's funny."

"I'm not saying it's funny, but the idea a silly inkwell could possibly know about every spell ever cast in Lemon Bliss seems far-fetched. I'm sure you don't have to worry about every spell being attributed to you."

I watched as she fretted, chewed on her bottom lip and wrung her hands. "A long time ago I cast a love spell and it ruined a man's life," she blurted out.

"Mom!" Daphne exclaimed.

"You did what?" I repeated.

Magnolia nodded her head. "I was young and stupid and very selfish. I didn't understand how potent a love spell could be. I fear I ruined the man's life."

"The man wasn't dad?" Daphne asked.

Magnolia gave a weak smile. "No, it wasn't your father."

"Who was it?" I asked, a little afraid to know the truth.

She let out a long sigh. "He was my boyfriend in high school. I was so in love with him, but he didn't feel the same. All the girls thought he was handsome and he was a horrible flirt. I was so worried he would dump me. I cast a love spell to ensure he would never leave me."

"But you didn't marry him?" I asked, a little confused.

She smiled. "No, he wasn't the man for me. It turned out he really was a shallow young man and despite the spell's effects, I realized I didn't love him. His family moved away, but he continued to write and call for years. I moved on and fell in love with Daphne's father."

"Where is this guy?" Daphne asked.

"I don't know for sure, but I do know he never married. He couldn't. To this day, I worry he's still in love with me, all because of that stupid spell," Magnolia said, shame evident in her voice.

"Why didn't you undo the spell?" I asked.

"I didn't know how. I was young and very naïve. None of us knew how, and I was too ashamed and afraid to ask the elder witches. I let that man go on like that for years," she whispered.

"Wow," I mumbled. "You guys sure did play fast and loose with magic back then. No wonder Daphne and I were kept in the dark for so long. It's amazing the four of you didn't land in prison," I said with a shake of my head.

Magnolia looked as if I had slapped her. I was annoyed and didn't care if it offended her. Here they were, constantly lecturing Daphne and I about what we could and couldn't do, only to find out they had done it all.

"It was a different time back then," Magnolia defended.

"Oh, back then it was okay to use and manipulate people and ruin any chance of happiness they may have in their lives?" I asked. "I think it's terrible. Once all of this business is taken care of, you need to find a way to release that poor man."

"I shouldn't have told you. I only wanted you to learn from my mistakes," she said, her gaze bouncing from me to Daphne. "I'll go."

"We'll learn alright, but honestly, I can't say a love spell is something I would ever consider. If a man doesn't love you, he doesn't love you. Period. No amount of magic is going to change that."

"I was young. I was a bit of an outcast, and I thought for sure he did love me, he just needed a little reminder," she said before walking out the door.

Daphne and I stood there staring at each other. She seemed to be taking the news a lot better than I was.

"Well, that was a bit of a bombshell, wasn't it?" Daphne said.

I slapped my palm against the counter. "I can't believe them! My word it's a miracle this place is still standing. All these lectures about being careful, and none of these messes we're been dealing with would have happened if they'd been more careful. Well, them and our ancestors."

Daphne nodded. "I get it, but maybe that's why they keep telling us to be careful. It seems like they have learned from their mistakes."

The bell jingled from out front, and she pushed through the swinging door. I settled in to make bread dough. The kneading would help me work through my frustration and irritation.

I mulled over Magnolia's confession. The women seemed to know their way around love spells. I smiled as an idea came to mind. We could cast a love spell on Daphne's cheating soon-to-be ex-husband. That would serve him right. He would fall head over heels in love with a woman who would never give him the time of day. The idea was very appealing. I could imagine the satisfaction it would bring Daphne to see the man who had hurt her so terribly suffer as she had.

I stopped the kneading.

What the hell, Violet?

That was not who I was. I was not someone who actively

sought revenge. I was definitely not the kind of person who thought about using magic to hurt someone. I needed to get my head straight. I didn't like my train of thought. I wouldn't let my mother and her friends lead me down a road that would leave me with far too many regrets.

CHAPTER 14

$\mathcal{I}$ climbed into Gabriel's truck, butterflies dancing in my belly.

"Are you sure you want to do this?" he asked me for what had to be the tenth time.

"Yes. I'm sure."

He exhaled a loud breath. "Fine. Let me do the talking. George knows me, and I have a feeling he'll be more inclined to talk to me."

I shrugged. "Fine, but if I see anything fishy or get any weird vibes, I'm going to demand he turn over the artifacts."

He smiled. "I know you will. Are you sure you don't want to swing by Harold's office and give him a heads up?"

"Absolutely not. The man is useless. The only thing on his mind is Lila these days. We can't rely on him to be of any assistance."

With a wry chuckle, Gabriel nodded and drove out of town, heading for the old property where George was residing. It had been a long time since I'd been out to this area. We drove by rolling fields interspersed with trees.

Gabriel turned down the winding dirt road that led to

the old home where George was staying, rolling his truck to a stop in front of the old farmhouse. "I'll do the talking," he reminded me in a low voice as we walked onto the tiny porch.

When George opened the door, my heart leapt. Despite my commitment to doing this, he made me nervous. I didn't know what to think about his alleged abilities to sniff out supernatural powers.

"Gabriel!" he greeted as if they were old friends. "What brings you out here?"

"Hi, George. I was hoping to talk to you for a minute about that business at the museum. I hear you have the missing chest," Gabriel said, diving right to the heart of the matter, taking me by surprise.

George surprised me further. "I do. It's sitting on my back porch in the same spot it's been since someone left it there," he said gesturing towards the back of the house. "I don't want to touch it. I told Sheriff Smith about it, but he didn't seem all that interested in getting it back. It's here for him to have."

"Can I see it?" I asked.

George eyed me up and down. "You're the one who owns that factory, aren't you?"

I nodded. "Yeah, I inherited the property from my grandmother."

His eyes narrowed. "You sure you don't know anything else about Dale's death?"

I returned his gaze. "You sure you don't since you were the one breaking and entering?"

After a tense moment, George looked away. Gabriel threw me a look that I interpreted as a *shut-the-hell-up* look. I shrugged. It was true. George has trespassed in the old factory.

"Fine, you can see it. It's back here. How did you know it was here?" George asked.

Oops. "Harold told me," I said. It was the truth after all. Kind of.

"Why would he tell you something like that?" he asked, clearly not buying my story.

I decided honesty was the best approach. "I overheard you two in the post office."

George shook his head, gesturing for us to follow. "I got nothing to hide. If you overheard me, you know it just showed up here." He walked us through the cabin and out a back door to a covered porch. In the corner, right by the single step off the porch sat the chest.

He paused, blocking us from going onto the porch. "Why do you want to see the chest?" he asked.

I looked at Gabriel, asking for help.

Gabriel grinned. "I was curious. There's a lot of mystery surrounding it, and I love antiques."

That seemed to placate George. He moved out of the way and let us pass.

"It's a peculiar thing," he said gesturing to the chest.

"Why do you have it?" I asked again.

He looked at me. "As I just said, it showed up here. I woke up one morning, went outside to have some coffee and there it was."

"Why would someone think to leave it with you?" I pressed.

"I couldn't say. You would have to ask that person, don't you think?" he asked with a sigh.

I took a deep breath. I wanted to throttle him. I didn't like him on principle alone. He was irritating and had an air about him that said he thought he was better than everyone else. I really didn't like him in the least. There was that and the reality he posed a threat to me and the other witches in Lemon Bliss. With all his nosing around, he'd stirred things up.

"Any idea how much this thing is worth?" I asked.

George shrugged. "Look at the thing. It's barely holding together. The only monetary value it holds is the wood. It would make a nice campfire, I suppose."

"You do know it is more than two hundred years old, right?"

He shrugged a shoulder. "That's the story, but who's here to dispute that?"

Gabriel reached for my hand, curling his around it. His strong, steady touch calmed me. I couldn't get into a battle of words with George. Not now.

"What about the other missing item?" I asked, not naming it. I wanted to test him to see if he knew more than he claimed.

He shrugged. "I have nothing else."

"What's the big deal about the chest anyway?" Gabriel asked, feigning innocence.

George smiled. "It's rumored to hold enchantments, kind of like a Pandora's box. Folks in the supernatural world have been gossiping about the idea of such a chest for years. Dale did some digging and according to his notes, this might be one of those chests."

Gabriel made a choking sound. I refused to look at him. Now he knew. "Really?" he murmured. "Did Dale actually find the chest?"

"No, unfortunately he died before he got the chance to lay eyes on it. He described it in detail in his notes though. I have all of his notebooks and whatnot about the investigation into supernatural happenings here in Lemon Bliss. I won't let his death be in vain. I'm picking up where he left off," he said as if he was some great hero.

I bit back my frustration and stayed quiet.

"That's nice of you," Gabriel said.

"I'm happy to do it. The network is thrilled to have the material to do another special."

I glanced to George, trying to gauge his reaction. He was

clearly excited. If he had more material to use in yet another episode on the supernatural world in Lemon Bliss, myself and my fellow witches were still at risk.

"The chest will be featured in this new special?" Gabriel asked.

"Yes! I read about it in Dale's notes. I received an anonymous tip the chest was on display at the local museum. I went to the museum to check it out and confirmed it was in fact the same chest Dale had referenced in his notes. You can imagine how sad I was to learn it had disappeared when I had just found it. Then, out of the blue, it appeared on my doorstep," he said, as if it was a miracle. "Now, I can move forward with the next episode!"

I didn't buy it. I turned back to the chest and stepped towards it, squatting down to get a closer look, but not touching it. I had no idea what would happen if I did. I most certainly didn't want to be the one who inadvertently released dark powers into the world.

"It doesn't bite," George quipped. "In fact, you can't even open it. I've tried."

My stomach churned. If he had managed to get past the lock, all kinds of crazy things could have been set in motion. At least according to my mother, that was. That was one boundary I wasn't willing to test. I was going to take her word for it.

I returned my focus to the chest and noticed the lid vibrating. I immediately stood and stepped back, looking up to see if Gabriel or George had noticed. They seemed to be involved in their own conversation. George was carrying on about the chest and how exciting it was to have discovered it right there in plain sight.

"Why haven't you taken it back to the museum or turned it in to the sheriff's office?" I asked.

George shrugged. "I don't want my fingerprints on it."

"You said you tried to open it," I reminded him.

"Well, yes, but I don't want to be caught with that thing. I don't know what powers it holds, but I would rather the sheriff come and pick it up. I've told him several times. Obviously, it isn't a big deal or he would have picked it up days ago," George explained.

Gabriel looked at me. "That does seem strange. He's been busy, lately," he said.

"We'll take it," I blurted out.

George shook his head. "No, you won't. That things stays right there until the sheriff comes to claim it."

"You said he knows it's here. He doesn't seem to think you took it. We'll give it to him, and he can close the investigation," I said.

"Nope. I'll only let the sheriff take it out of here."

I nearly growled in frustration. Gabriel shot me a look.

"Okay, we better head out. Thanks for letting us take a look at it. It's a cool piece of history. I don't know if I believe it is supernatural, but the woodwork and carvings are remarkable," Gabriel said.

I rolled my eyes, considered grabbing the chest and making a run for it, but I was afraid it would jostle open. I didn't need to be the one blamed for ruining the world. That wasn't a risk I was willing to take.

The moment we got into the truck and George had disappeared inside the cabin, Gabriel turned to look at me. "What was that about?"

"What?" I asked, hoping it wasn't what I thought it was.

"I saw that chest vibrate when you got close."

"Oh. That. I don't know for sure," I said. I genuinely didn't know.

He stared at me for several long seconds. "Violet, that thing sensed you. It was basically asking you to open it. Is what George said true?"

"Gabriel, I know almost nothing about that chest. I know it shouldn't be opened. That's it."

I got the feeling he didn't believe me, which wasn't surprising. He knew I'd been holding back, and this was just another thing I couldn't talk to him about.

He backed out of the driveway and headed back into town. I knew he was thinking about what we saw. So was I. I needed to talk to my mom. I hoped she would be honest with me. I had the impression they hadn't told us everything about the chest, which irritated me. Withholding information was putting all of us at risk.

"Do you want to come in?" I asked him when we arrived at the house.

He shook his head. "No, I need to take care of a few things."

"Things?" I teased.

He looked at me. "Yes, things. We don't have to tell each other everything, do we?"

His comment stung a little, but I was the one holding back, so it wasn't fair for me to get annoyed. "Fine. I'll call you later?"

"Sure."

Slumping down on the couch a few minutes later, I sighed. The last thing I needed was a rocky relationship. My mother and her friends may enjoy the single life, but I had hoped for happily ever after at some point in my life. I didn't know if it would be with Gabriel, but I knew any man would want to know who I was. I couldn't keep up with keeping secrets forever.

CHAPTER 15

*N*ot much later, I called my mother.

"Hello, dear," she answered, sounding more like herself than she had in a while.

"Hi, Mom. I need to talk to you. To everyone," I said.

"Has something happened?" she asked, worry in her voice.

"No, but I paid George Cannon a visit."

"Oh. Oh, goodness. All right. We'll talk tonight. I'll call everyone else. Let's make it earlier than usual, say nine?"

"Works for me," I said, hanging up.

I felt a little better, knowing I could talk to the other witches. I was a little nervous to see Magnolia after our exchange earlier. I might've been harsh. While I still felt I had every right to be angry, I probably should have held my tongue. I had always been taught to respect my elders. I would apologize for my reaction, but I was still frustrated with the chain of events. So many problems could have been avoided.

I made myself something to eat, put in a load of laundry and tidied up before heading to the factory. I was glad the meeting was early. It meant I could get a full night's sleep and be prepared for what was to be a busy day tomorrow. We had our first big order for a business group. They had ordered a variety of cookies, muffins and a large cake for a banquet being held in Ruby Red. The fact they had chosen our little bakery over the bakeries in Ruby Red was a big deal. We couldn't afford to mess it up.

When I arrived at the factory alone, it felt strange. I always came with someone. Daphne hadn't called to ask if I wanted to carpool. I had a feeling she was a little upset with me over my reaction to her mother earlier.

I made my way into the factory. "Hi," my mother said, meeting me at the bottom of the stairs. Everyone else was already seated.

"Hi. Am I late?" I asked.

"No, no. We were all early."

I nodded, not moving into the room. "Am I in trouble? I'm guessing you didn't all sit here and stare at each other. I was the topic of the conversation, right?"

She shrugged a shoulder. "We're all under a lot of stress. It's understandable."

"Actually, it isn't. I need to apologize to Magnolia, but I won't apologize for getting frustrated. With everything going on, it's difficult to realize a lot of this could have been avoided. With y'all lecturing us about being careful with magic, we're in the middle of the mess because of others who weren't."

She patted my shoulder. "I know. We'll talk about all of that soon enough. One problem at a time."

I walked into the magically hidden room and flopped down in a vacant chair. "I went to George Cannon's place today and asked for the chest," I offered by way of greeting.

"You did what!" Lila gasped.

Daphne looked at me, her eyes widening. "With Gabriel. That's what you two were arguing about today."

"You took Gabriel?" Coral said in an accusatory tone.

"Actually, Gabriel took me. I told him what I planned to do, and he insisted on coming with me. He's fine. He didn't get zapped or turned into a toad or anything. Nothing nefarious happened," I said with a sigh.

Coral simply shook her head, her gaze accusing.

My mother stepped in to save me from what appeared to be a supernatural firing squad. "Did he give you the chest?"

"No. But I did see it. He told me he tried to open it."

A few gasps and looks of shock met my statement. "Did he open it?" Magnolia asked.

"No. He couldn't."

"He couldn't because it will only open for witches," my mother explained.

"When I got close to it, the lid vibrated. I immediately backed away," I added.

"It sensed your powers. If you had touched it, you would have been unable to resist opening it. It has a force few witches have the power to deny," Lila explained.

I had sensed the need to touch it, but I'd had enough of a clue to back away. I was relieved I had chosen to listen to that little voice of reason.

Moving on, I told them about the rest of my encounter and George's unequivocal denial he had anything to do with the actual theft. That led us back to Darlene and Rosa and their interest in the chest. Daphne filled them in on what we'd seen in the security videotapes.

"I did a little investigating. Darlene is actually a descendant of one of the founding families in Lemon Bliss," Magnolia added.

"That would explain her interest in the chest, or at least her knowledge of it," Coral said.

"We still know nothing about Rosa," Lila commented. "No one around town seems to know her."

"That's strange in itself," my mother stated.

"I asked George if any of the other missing artifacts had shown up on his porch, but he denied it. He didn't offer up if he knew what the other missing items were. I didn't get the feeling he had the inkwell, which means it's still out there somewhere," I said, a little disappointed I hadn't been able to find it. The inkwell seemed to be more of a threat than the chest at the moment.

"The inkwell has to be found!" Coral stressed.

"Let's focus on the chest. We know where it is. We could cast a cloaking spell and walk right in and take it back," Magnolia offered.

"No! That will trigger that nasty inkwell," Lila exclaimed.

"If it's sitting outside on that man's porch, it's not safe. Anyone could take it. I'm sure the entire supernatural world knows about our little problem. If one of the dark witches finds out that chest is unguarded, it will be up for grabs," my mom added.

I had to agree with that. It didn't make sense to leave the chest exposed when it was an easy enough job to grab it and run. George couldn't spend every minute of every day at the cabin.

"Why don't we ask Gabriel to take George to lunch?" Daphne offered.

"Sounds like I plan," I replied.

"No. When George discovers the chest missing, he's going to know Gabriel was in on it," Coral argued.

"So?" I shot back. "He wouldn't be able to prove it."

"I don't want my nephew involved," she huffed.

"He already is. He wants to help. Why not let him do this one thing?" I asked.

Everyone was silent.

"Maybe a better idea would be to have Lila convince Harold she wants the chest. He's under her spell and will do just anything to make her happy," Magnolia suggested.

I thought the idea was great, but clearly my opinion

didn't hold a lot of weight. I waited to say anything until someone else did first.

"I could do that," Lila said with a smile. "He won't question it at all. Virginia," she said, turning to look at my mother. "What do you think?"

"I think it could work. It isn't like he would be doing anything he wouldn't normally do. According to Violet, George has asked Harold to pick it up. I think it's the best plan yet," she said with a smile. "Coral, what do you think?"

Coral didn't look pleased, but she nodded her head in agreement. My mom looked to me, then Daphne. "And you two?"

"I think it's great," I said.

"Me too," Daphne added.

"Good, then it's settled. Lila, when do you think you can make it happen?" my mother asked.

"We're having lunch tomorrow. I'll ask him then," she said.

My mom clapped her hands together and stood. "Great!"

"What about the inkwell?" I asked.

"We keep looking. I'm going to do some more digging into Darlene's family," Magnolia answered.

It wasn't exactly what I wanted to hear, but I was willing to wait.

"Virginia, do we have a plan in case the inkwell manages to expose our coven?" Daphne asked.

The look on the faces of all the women said it all. There wasn't a plan. They had no idea how to handle it if that happened. That was scary.

"Being a witch isn't illegal, is it?" I asked, truly not sure.

"No, but it would certainly bring a great deal of scrutiny. Our entire lives would change. We would be hounded by those who were curious and those who saw us as evil and in need of extermination. There may not be witch trials like the kind they had in Salem, but we would most definitely be persecuted," Coral answered.

"Everything we know and love would be threatened," Magnolia whispered. "I hate to say it, but you girls would likely suffer far more than us. We can fade away and live out our lives, but the two of you, you stand to lose a great deal more."

Lovely. That wasn't ominous at all.

"Perfect. On that note, I'm going home to bed. I'm sure I'll sleep great tonight," I grumbled as I stood and walked to the stairs.

"Violet?" my mom called out, stopping me.

I turned to see what she needed. She nodded towards Magnolia.

Oh right. I'd planned to apologize to Magnolia. Spinning back, I walked over to her.

"Magnolia?"

She looked up at me, the concern in her eyes apparent. It pulled at my heartstrings. Magnolia was kind and loving and like an aunt to me.

"I'm sorry for being so harsh earlier. I was feeling cranky and I spoke without thinking," I said quietly.

A soft smile crossed her lips. "You were right. We were reckless back then. Our mothers warned us, but we didn't listen. I wished I had. Every single day I regret what I did to that man."

"Can it be undone?" I asked hopefully.

"I've tried. So many times, I tried to undo the spell. Nothing has worked."

"Oh. Does that mean Harold will always be this way with Lila?" I asked, shocked to know the infatuation could be a permanent affliction.

"Maybe."

"That can't be. We have to find a way to reverse the spell.

Once all of this is over and done, we will find a way to set things right," I vowed.

She smiled. "That's assuming we manage to deal with all of this."

"We will. I know it will work out. We'll get that chest and inkwell back and hide them where no one can find them. Go home and get some rest," I said firmly.

On the drive home, I considered where I could learn more about spells. It wasn't exactly something I could search online, but I knew there had to be a way to reverse a spell. I couldn't imagine witches around the world had never figured it out. If only there were some kind of witch network.

An idea sprang to mind. It would have to wait until Sunday when I had a day off, but I was confident I could come up with a solution for Magnolia's problem as well as Lila's.

CHAPTER 16

$\mathcal{O}$ur first big order was a huge success. After their event went off without a hitch and our bakery goods were a hit, the company called us with thanks. They also promised to send more business our way and to use us for any future events.

Since I'd experienced success once already with my first bakery, I knew I could do a good job, but every compliment was still thrilling. Gabriel and I were going out for a congratulatory dinner tomorrow night.

I practically bounced into the post office to check my mail. I had to mail a package to Tara as well. I had forgotten to mail it for days. She was busy doing a bang up job managing the bakery I'd left behind, and I'd meant to send her a thank you gift. To make sure I didn't miss it again, I intended to walk straight to the counter, but my phone insistent vibration in my pocket interrupted me. Slipping it out, I glanced down to see my mother's number on the screen.

My phone had been buzzing all day with texts. My mother was the go-between for everyone and had been keeping us updated on Project Steal the Chest back. So far, it was all going off without a hitch, which was another reason for my good mood. I tucked my phone back into my pocket and walked to the counter, presenting my package.

"Hi," I said, greeting the postal clerk who had her back to me.

She turned around and didn't look all that happy to see me. I realized it was near closing time, but it wasn't like I was mailing twenty packages. It would only take a minute of her time.

"Can I help you?" she asked, her tone flat.

I smiled, hoping to warm her up. My eyes moved to her nametag. Darlene. I looked up at her face and connected the dots. She was the same postal clerk who'd been giving me the side eye when I'd been eavesdropping on Harold and George. She was also one of the women in the security videos from the museum. Darlene Clayton was standing right in front of me. *How come no one had mentioned she worked at the post office?*

"I need to mail this," I said, my mind whirring. This was my chance to talk with her. I was not big on small talk. I didn't chat up strangers, but I needed to know who this woman was. If I were friendly, maybe she would spill all her deep, dark secrets. For example, why she stole the artifacts from the museum. A girl can hope, right?

She snatched the package from my hand, put it on a scale and punched some keys on her keyboard.

"Have you worked here long?" I asked, hoping to get her talking.

"A year."

Not exactly a chatty Kathy.

"Do you like working here? I bet you get to meet lots of the locals, huh?"

She looked up at me. "It's a job. It pays the bills."

124

"I own the new bakery that just opened up down the road."

"Congratulations," she mumbled.

I bit back a sardonic laugh. No one would ever say she was enthusiastic.

"Thanks. It's going well." I hoped my quite obvious attempt to make conversation would encourage her to talk.

I looked around the post office. It was empty. It was a good time to try and pull some information from her. Darlene *was* going to chat with me if I had to pry information out of her.

"What brought you to Lemon Bliss?" I questioned.

She stopped what she was doing and looked at me. "I like it here."

"Oh, really. Did you visit here before you decided to move here? I mean, Lemon Bliss isn't exactly a place people know about."

Darlene went back to her work on the computer. Within seconds, the printer spit out a label, which she slapped on my little box.

She released a long sigh, and I hoped I had finally cracked her frosty shell. "My great-great grandparents lived here. She's buried in the local cemetery. I was at a point in my life where a move seemed like a good idea," she explained. "When I was younger, I used to visit a lot and this place reminded me of better times."

I nodded, understanding more than she knew. I assumed she was on the run from the business in New York. What better place to hideout than a little town in southern Louisiana where people minded their own business and left folks alone. Maybe she had skipped out on bail or avoided arrest by fleeing.

"It's a nice place," I confirmed. "I like it."

"What about you? Why are you back?" she asked.

That caught me by surprise. She didn't know me. How

would she know I was back? "Did we go to school togeth-er?" I asked curiously, already knowing the answer. "I didn't realize we knew each other."

"No, I didn't live here when you did, and we don't know each other," she said haughtily.

"But you know I'm back. Do you know who I am?" I asked, deciding to forgo being polite at this point.

I wanted information, but she was rude.

She held up the package and pointed to the return address. "You're Violet Broussard."

"Oh, duh," I giggled, feeling a little stupid for jumping to conclusions. "I don't think we've ever met, have we? Which is strange in a town this small. I guess I don't mail a lot of stuff."

She shook her head. "No, we've never met, not outside of here. I know your family's name and let's face it, your family is kind of a big deal around here. You're like a super star or something," she said sarcastically.

"Oh. So, you know my mother?"

I could tell she was getting frustrated with my questions.

"No, I don't. My ancestors knew your ancestors. There were stories passed down through the generations. I know of your family, not any of you personally. Like I said, people gossip. I'm in a position where I hear a lot of stuff and your name has come up once or twice."

"Oh, I see. Well I hope the stories were good," I teased.

The way she was looking at me made me question that idea. My witch radar was blaring. Something was off. Darlene was looking at me with something close to malice. It was unnerving.

I didn't get a chance to press her further. She was looking past me. Turning to see what had caught her attention, I spotted Rosa staring at my back. I recognized her by the cane and grainy image on the surveillance video.

"Hi. I'm just about finished," I said, suddenly wanting to get out of the post office.

The two women were staring at each as if they were communicating without words. It was spooky. I felt like I was in the middle of a quarrel. A silent quarrel, but nonetheless.

"No worries. Take your time," Rosa said from behind me with a tight smile.

"Thanks," I murmured, turning back to face Darlene, who was shooting daggers at poor Rosa.

"That's it. That's all I need," I said quickly, digging in my purse for some cash.

"You sure you don't want stamps or something?" Darlene asked in a cold tone.

"Nope. I'm good. Just that, thanks."

I quickly paid, thanked Darlene and turned to leave. Rosa was intently staring at me. Typically, I would stare back at a person acting so rudely, but with her, I couldn't. I was afraid to look directly into her eyes.

For some reason, an inner voice told me I should, under no circumstances, challenge the rather diminutive woman before me. I was physically bigger, but she was a scary little thing. I was starting to regret my decision to come into the post office. I should have paid and left, but no, I had to get all snoopy and play private detective.

I took a deep breath. "I just need to check my mail," I said, thankful for an excuse to get away from the standoff unfolding. Once Rosa was at the counter, I turned away, walking toward the post office boxes.

"Your house is beautiful," Rosa blurted out.

My heart kicked up a notch as did my anxiety level. "Pardon?" I squeaked out.

"I mean, the flowers. Your grandmother's flowers are always so beautiful. I love to stop by and look at them," she clarified.

It didn't make the comment any less strange. "Oh, thank you. Did you know my grandmother?"

She shrugged a dainty shoulder. "I knew of her. We met once or twice."

"Oh, I didn't realize you had lived here that long. I don't think we've ever met before."

She shook her head. "No, not formally."

"Well, I'm Violet Broussard," I said, keeping my hands close to my body. I was too afraid to touch her. I had the feeling she would zap me.

"Rosa Herrera. It's nice to meet you."

Her words were directed at me, but her gaze was on Darlene.

"Okay, well I should get my mail and get out of here, so Darlene can close up," I said, stepping to the side and heading back towards the wall of mailboxes.

I could feel their eyes on me as I walked away. The hair on the back of my neck rose.

CHAPTER 17

*M*y mouth was dry, and my hands were shaking by the time I got to my box. Darlene and Rosa had unnerved me. I didn't like it one bit. I struggled to get the key into the small door.

I could hear their shushed, hurried voices on the other side of the mailboxes. I froze, cocked my head to the side and listened. I strained to hear what they were saying, but I couldn't make out the words. Whatever it was, they both sounded angry. I wasn't sure if they were angry with me, or with each other.

I opened my box, grabbed my mail and rushed out the door, hoping they wouldn't notice. From my car in front of the windows of the post office, I could see them talking. Rosa was gesturing wildly.

My hopes they weren't talking about me were dashed when Rosa turned to point directly at me. I started my car and took off towards home. My earlier cheery mood vanished into my worries. When I reached the safety of my home, I went inside and locked the door. It was silly. I knew that, but I did it anyway.

Grabbing a glass of wine, I plopped down on the couch to go through the mail.

"Oh no," I muttered, holding the tiny scrap of paper. "Oh crap."

It was a note from the inkwell.

"All witches have been called out. Exposure is imminent."

My heart sank. I knew none of the witches in my coven had cast a spell to call out witches. There must be another witch in town who had cast this spell. That was the only explanation. Sweet tea!

I jumped up and reached for my phone.

"Daphne! I got a note!" I screeched the second she answered.

"What?" she yelled into the phone.

"Yes! This is not good. What am I going to do?"

"I'll be right over," she said, hanging up.

I paced the living room, reading the note over and over. I had to tell my mom. I didn't want to tell her, but I had to. I knew this meant an emergency meeting. I was not interested in heading off to the factory. The feeling of being watched earlier was real. Someone knew.

Daphne was pounding on my door five minutes later. I yanked it open.

"Where is it?" she asked.

I handed her the note. "What does that mean?" I said frantically.

She was shaking her head. "I don't know, but it can't be good. Nothing good can come of this."

"Who cast the spell?"

"It wasn't me. I doubt it was any of us. George?" she suggested.

"I don't know. This is awful. If a spell called out all witches, what are we going to do? Gah! I wish I didn't know I was a witch. Then, I could be oblivious."

Daphne ran a hand through her hair. "This is bad."

I nodded in agreement. "We have to tell the others."

The doorbell rang, but whoever was there didn't wait for me to open it. It was my mother. She pushed in, followed by Lila and Magnolia.

"What is it?" Lila asked. "Where is it?"

Magnolia moved to shut the door, but stopped when Coral came rushing through.

I stared at the crowd in my living room, my mouth agape. "How did you all know?"

Daphne looked embarrassed. "I called Mom, who I assume called everyone else."

"She should have called us. This is horrifying," Coral said, taking the note that was being passed around the room.

"What do we do?" I asked, looked to my mom for guidance. "Who cast that spell?"

"I don't know. We'll figure it out. Everyone," she said, clapping her hands like a teacher calling students to attention. "Everyone take a seat. We'll work through this. Relax."

We all squished together on the couch. The tension in the air was palpable.

"Should we all be meeting here, like this?" I asked. It was more than evident we were being watched. This impromptu gathering was sure to raise suspicions.

"We won't stay long," Coral replied.

"What do we do?" Daphne asked. "What does it mean they called out all the witches?"

My mother waved her hand. "It's a spell that will reveal our true identities. Everyone we meet will see us for witches. I imagine many people will be afraid, some will hate us and some will want to be our best friends."

"It's a dangerous spell. Our secrets will be laid bare for the world to see. It isn't just us. Witches from all around the area will be exposed. Those that have been living in the shadows will have a spotlight shown on them," Magnolia fretted.

"How will they know?" I asked, truly wondering how anyone can determine a person's witchy status by looking at them.

My mother and Magnolia exchanged a look. "We will appear as the traditional witch in fairytales."

Daphne gasped. "No! You mean huge noses and warts?"

Magnolia nodded her head slowly.

"No! Everyone will see us like that?" I asked, horrified and immediately wondering what Gabriel would see when he looked at me. The customers at the bakery would never want to come in and buy cookies from a couple of terrifying witches.

"We must stop this," Coral said firmly.

I enthusiastically agreed.

"Other witches will see us for who we are," Lila added. "You will still look the same to me and vice versa."

"Thanks, but that doesn't exactly make me feel better," I quipped.

"On a good note, Harold will be picking up the chest tomorrow morning," Lila announced.

"Thank goodness," my mother breathed out.

Daphne scoffed. "As if that matters if everyone knows who the witches in this town are."

"It will help. We can protect the world from the evils sealed in that chest," Coral said firmly.

"I need to get going," Lila announced. "Harold will be at my house shortly. I plan on asking him to leave me the chest for safekeeping."

"You're leaving?" I asked in shock. "We may all be exposed and you're going to leave?"

She smiled. "Sweetie, we are not the first witches to face

this particular crisis. In fact, you will find this tends to be something all witches face every day. Will we be exposed or will we be safe? I have faith your mother and the rest of you smart ladies will figure something out. I have to take care of this other little problem."

She walked out of the house. Coral stood and announced she too needed to leave.

When she left, I felt as if we had been abandoned. They were jumping ship, and it was the four of us left holding the bag, assuming no one else left.

"Now what?" I asked.

"Now, we think," my mother answered. "There has to be another witch living among us. We know we didn't cast that spell."

"What about that Darlene woman?" I asked. "I just had a very creepy run-in with her at the post office. That woman is scary."

"How? What did she do?" Magnolia asked.

I shrugged and gave them an accounting of our brief meeting.

Daphne nodded along. "That's how she is with me. She's never nice."

"I don't know that I know her family. The name isn't familiar," my mom said, looking thoughtful. "She insisted her ancestors were part of the founding families of Lemon Bliss?"

I nodded. "Yes. She was very weird about it. I felt like she had been stalking me. And then Rosa Herrera showed up. Whatever is between those two women is even stranger. I felt like they wanted to kill each other, but were also best friends if that makes any sense."

"Great, as if we need any more people who don't like us," Daphne mumbled.

"I think we need to start with this Darlene Clayton. If

she has some kind of animosity towards the Broussard family, she is very likely the one who's trying to expose us. Back in the old days, witchcraft was suspected quite often. I imagine my great-grandmother and her mother were suspected of being witches. Anyone who did anything out of the ordinary back then was accused of being a witch," my mother said, appearing much calmer than she had five minutes ago.

Daphne smirked. "Maybe your great grammy hexed her great grammy or stole her man," she joked.

I laughed. "You know, sadly, that's probably what happened. A hundred years later and we get to pay the price for their foolishness."

"Back then, anything was possible," my mother offered. "They were far more likely to dance naked in the bayou or practice magic right in their own kitchens. I know the Broussard women come from a long line of proud witches who have never tried to hide who they were. It wasn't until my mother that things started to change. She encouraged the witches in the coven to try and blend in with society."

"Can't we just confront this Darlene woman?" Daphne asked.

"No!" Magnolia said vehemently. "If she's a witch, she may have tapped into the darkness. She could hurt you or worse. Let Virginia and I do some digging in the family archives. We'll see if we can find her family's name."

"What if the name is different? Her grandmother may have married and so on down the line?"

My mother nodded her head. "You're right. Can you search online to find out?"

I chuckled. My mother hated computers and turned to me for just about anything to do with them. "Yes, I can try to see what we can dig up online, but people use fake names all the time."

"That's true. Wait!" Daphne said excitedly. "I bought a

subscription to some background check service a while back. It should still be active. We can use it to look her up."

I raised an eyebrow. "Have you been running background checks on people?"

She smirked. "My ex and a couple of the women I caught him cheating with."

"Oh," I murmured in understanding. "Well, good, we'll start there. Can you use my laptop to get into the system?"

"Yep."

My mother stood and looked to Magnolia who followed her lead. "You girls do that. We're headed to the factory to dig through some of the old books there. If you find a maiden name different than Clayton, call us," she said.

"We will," I said, before racing upstairs to grab the computer.

By the time I got back downstairs, I could hear Daphne in the kitchen.

"Hungry?" I asked her, coming in behind her.

"I need wine. Please tell me you have a bottle stashed around here."

I chuckled. "Hello? Do you know who you're talking to here?"

That made her giggle. In that moment, things were okay. I wasn't afraid to walk down the street with everyone pointing at the giant wart on my nose. We could get through this.

I reached into the cupboard over the refrigerator and pulled out a bottle.

"Ha! I knew you would hide it."

"It's my emergency stash. I'll grab a couple glasses. Go sit down and let's see what we can hunt up on Darlene. If she's messing with my life, I want to take her down!"

Daphne grabbed the laptop and sat at the kitchen table, quickly tapping on the keys. I delivered the bottle of wine, filled two glasses and waited. My stomach twisted in knots as I thought of the many possibilities. One of them being the fact we might not be able to find much more than I already had on Darlene.

"Got her!" Daphne announced, a huge smile spreading across her face. "We got you now," she said, staring at the screen.

She turned the laptop so I could see. "Dunshire?" I asked looking at her mother's maiden name.

Daphne stood and hurried to the living room and at the couch to grab her purse and phone. I scanned the screen while she called her mom to relay what we'd found.

When she came back to the table, she was grinning. "Your mom recognizes the name. They're going to do some digging."

"Good. I wonder what happened?" I mused out loud. "I mean, what did my ancestors do to her ancestors to make her hate us so much?"

Daphne rolled her eyes. "I seriously wouldn't be surprised if it was over a man. Some things never change."

"If it turns out to be Darlene who cast the spell, doesn't she realize that will expose her as well?"

"Maybe she did some kind of cloaking thing that hides her true identity. Who knows why people do what they do?" she mused, shaking her head.

"I don't know, but I'm looking forward to all of this being over. I guess we can assume she has the inkwell too."

Daphne looked thoughtful. "She might not. Or maybe she has it and doesn't realize it would tattle on her for casting that spell."

"My head is spinning. I don't want to think about what ifs anymore. We'll wait and see what our moms figure out."

Daphne stood up, stretched and announced she was leaving.

"I'll talk to you tomorrow," I told her, realizing it was

still early, but I was looking forward to a hot bubble bath and an early bedtime.

"See ya," she said and headed out the door.

I locked it behind her and shut off the lights before heading upstairs. I hoped we were close to the end of the whole debacle. Then, maybe I could relax again.

CHAPTER 18

*M*y mother and the rest of her friends were busy with the witch hunt. They assured me I didn't need to worry. The spell to call out witches hadn't worked. It was a false alarm, or a mean joke. I could go out to dinner with Gabriel without fear of him or anyone else seeing me as an ugly old hag. So they said. I was still feeling a little trepidation about the whole thing.

I had just finished getting ready when I heard the doorbell.

"Come in!" I called down the stairs, knowing it would be Gabriel.

I heard the door open and then close.

"I'll be right down!" I hollered before reaching into the closet to grab my heels.

I froze when I didn't hear a response.

"Gabriel?" I said, doing my best to hide the fear in my voice.

I waited, my heart beating like a drum. I held my breath, waiting for him to announce his presence. I grabbed one of my pointy-heeled shoes and prepared to attack whoever my intruder was.

"It's me," his voice called out.

I nearly collapsed in relief. I wanted to yell at him for scaring me, but it had all been in my head. He had done nothing.

I hurried downstairs to find him sitting on the couch. "I'm ready," I announced.

"Great. You look beautiful," he said, kissing me gently on the forehead.

He had no idea how much those words meant to me. I had been terrified the spell would kick in as I walked down the stairs, and he would see a frightening witch, pointy hat and all.

"Ready?" he asked.

"Yep, starving."

We headed out to his truck.

"Who's that?" he asked, pointing to a car parked on the other side of the road. I looked through the driver's window and saw Darlene staring back at me.

"Darlene Clayton," I said, my throat going dry.

"Why is she here?"

"I don't know, but let's get out of here. She freaks me out," I said, walking a little faster towards his truck.

"Want me to tell her to get lost?"

"It's a public road."

I wanted to tell him all about her, but not now. Tonight was supposed to be fun and the last thing I wanted to think about was an evil witch seeking revenge on my family for some ancient problem I knew nothing about.

By the time we arrived at the restaurant in Ruby Red, my nerves had calmed. I was ready for an enjoyable evening with Gabriel. It had been just that until towards the end of our meal I spotted Rosa. She was at another table, watching us.

I pretended not to see her. I didn't want to alarm Gabriel.

"Finished?" I asked, tossing my napkin on the table.

"Sure. Are you okay?"

"I'm good. I'm just a little tired. I think I may be coming down with something," I said, hoping my excuse would work.

"Oh, I'm sorry. We'll go," he said, motioning for the check.

As we walked out of the restaurant, I could feel Rosa's eyes on me. It was unnerving, but I refused to let it show. The women were not going to intimidate me. I sensed that was what they were after. They wanted me on edge so I would screw up and say or do something that would incriminate me as a witch.

Gabriel dropped me off. Thankfully, he bought my story that I wasn't feeling well and didn't ask to come in. We were just settling back to a sort of normal vibe after I'd had to keep a few witchy secrets from him. Of course, *normal* in my new life as a witch in Lemon Bliss wasn't the usual normal.

I locked the door behind him and quickly went to my room. I wanted to crawl under the covers and hide from the prying eyes I felt all around me. I had just changed into my pajamas when I heard a noise downstairs. I froze, scanning the dark room as I looked for something to arm myself with. I found nothing that gave me any real comfort and decided to wing it.

I silently crept downstairs. The living room was completely dark. I waited, listening for sounds indicating someone was inside.

Nothing.

I walked down a little further and still heard nothing. I flipped a switch, flooding the area with light. There was no one there. My shoulders sagged with relief, but it was short-lived. I heard a noise on my front porch and quickly rushed to the door, undid the lock and swung it open.

"Stop!" I yelled at the figure dashing into the darkness.

I nearly tripped over the chest as I raced out the door. That would have to wait. I recognized the figure hobbling down the pathway.

"Stop!" I yelled again. "Rosa, stop!"

The woman stopped running and turned to face me. "Stay away!" she yelled.

I stepped closer to her, hoping to have a rational conversation with her. The next thing I knew she hit me on the shoulder with her cane.

"Ow!" I yelped, taking a step back and stepping directly onto a jagged rock, the rock scraping my bare foot.

Rosa pursued me and whacked me with her cane against my left shin. Even though I cried out, Rosa kept at me with her cane. Seconds later, I saw the cane fly through the air.

"That's enough!" I heard Daphne's voice cut through the cool night air.

Rosa dropped to her knees and sobbed. "I'm sorry," she wailed.

I managed to straighten up, my body throbbing from where she had whacked at me with her cane.

"What are you doing here?" I asked Daphne who rushed towards me.

"Long story, but the real question is, what in the world is going on?"

I shook my head. "I have no idea. You would have to ask her," I said, turning to glare at Rosa who was still sobbing. You'd have thought I'd been beating her with a cane, instead of the other way around.

"I should call the sheriff," Daphne said, pulling her phone out of her back pocket.

"No! No! Please! I'm sorry," Rosa repeated.

"Why shouldn't we call the police?" I asked.

It was then I realized Daphne had used her powers to rip the cane out of Rosa's hands. I turned to look at her and smiled. "Nice move."

She grinned. "Thanks. My mom said our powers feed off our emotions," she whispered.

Rosa slowly stood up. "I'm sorry. I only wanted to bring you the chest. When you chased me, I panicked."

"The chest?" Daphne asked.

I nodded, recalling that I tripped over it when I took off after her.

"Yes, I brought the chest."

"Rosa, why do you have the chest?" I asked, my anger fading.

"I took it," she answered. "Not from the museum. I took it from Darlene," she clarified. Her earlier distress seemed to be lessening.

Daphne was shaking her head. "What a mess. We need to get you inside and take a look to make sure you aren't seriously hurt. I'll call your mom to help us sort through this."

I nodded in agreement. My feet hurt and every inch of my body felt like it was throbbing.

I looked at Rosa, picking up her cane. "Can you walk without it?"

"Yes, not easily, but I can manage."

"Good, I'm holding onto this. Let's go inside and you can tell us why you had the chest in the first place."

"I didn't have it," she said again. "Darlene had it."

"Fine, you can tell us why Darlene had it," I grumbled. I was not in the best mood, what with getting scared in my own house and beaten with a cane. The only saving grace was Rosa didn't swing her cane very hard.

I could hear Daphne talking as we walked back to the house. I briefly considered whacking Rosa just once with her own cane to give her a taste of her own medicine, but knew that was pointless.

"Sit," Daphne instructed, pointing to the couch once we were inside. "I'll grab some ice." She turned to look at Rosa. "You sit right there. You move and trust me, you'll regret it," she warned.

Rosa sat down in one of the chairs and quietly waited. Daphne came back with a bag of ice and a bag of frozen peas.

It wasn't long before my mother showed up. When she saw me resting on the couch with my sore leg propped up on the coffee table, the peas draped over my shin, she went into mother-mode, clucking and fussing as she looked me over.

When she decided I would live, she spun around, hands on her hips and glared at Rosa. "Explain yourself!"

"I'm sorry. I didn't mean to hurt her," Rosa started. "I only wanted the chest returned."

"Why did you have it?" my mother asked.

"I took it from Darlene. Darlene stole it."

"Why did she steal it and how did you know? Did you help her?" I asked.

"No! I saw her one night. I often take strolls at night. I enjoy the night walks. I saw her taking the chest from the museum. I questioned her, but she told me it was none of my business," she explained.

"Why would Darlene want the chest?" Daphne asked.

Rosa looked down at her hands. "She hates your families. She blames you for her family's ruin. She says you stole her inheritance and ruined their lives."

"That seems a little dramatic. How could have done that?"

Rosa looked up and stared directly into my mother's eyes. "Your ancestors cursed her ancestors. They bound their powers, preventing them from being able to practice magic."

Daphne and I glanced to each other, our wide gazes

colliding. My mother didn't look all that surprised to hear this revelation.

"I thought as much. There's an entry in our family tomes about a witch who regularly practiced in the dark arts. My ancestors and other members of the coven bound the powers of the ones guilty of using their magic for evil," she said.

Rosa nodded her head. "Yes. She wants revenge. She says it's her right to use magic, but because of the curse, she can't. According to Darlene, that binding spell ruined their family. They lost everything."

My mom shook her head, her eyes narrowing. "They gained wealth by using dark magic! Of course they lost it all."

Rosa shook her head. "I'm sorry. I told her to return the items. She threatened me if I told. She couldn't open the chest. She told me she gave it to that supernatural investigator so he could find a way to open it."

"Well that was useless," I mumbled.

"I didn't know what she planned to do, I swear. I thought she was stealing the items to sell. I had no idea she was a witch, or that you were witches," Rosa said, her voice trembling. "I don't want any trouble. I only wanted to settle this before someone got hurt. Darlene scares me. I have no idea what she may do."

"You did the right thing," my mother said, placing a hand on her shoulder. "Thank you. Now, we must figure out what to do next."

"Mom, um, don't we have a bit of a problem here?" I asked, looking at Rosa.

My mother waved a hand at me, her bracelets clinking with the movement. "Not now, dear."

"Does Darlene have anything else?" my mother pressed.

Rosa looked up at her and nodded. "Yes."

"That's what I thought."

Everything started to make sense.

"Daphne, keep an eye on these two. I need to make a quick phone call," my mother said and walked outside.

The three of us looked at each other.

"I'm sorry about your leg," Rosa said quietly. "And your shoulder."

"I'm fine. I'll survive."

Daphne glared at Rosa. "You shouldn't hit people."

I had to laugh. The night had certainly taken a very strange turn. Here I thought I was going to go to be early and sleep in the following day.

I should have known life would have other plans.

CHAPTER 19

I leaned my head back against the couch, waiting for my mother to return. A thought sprang to mind, and I turned to look at Daphne who was still eyeballing Rosa as if she would jump out and attack.

"How did you know to come save me?" I asked her.

She giggled. "I didn't know I was going to be saving you when I headed over. I ran into Gabriel at the gas station. He was picking up a six-pack of beer, and I was scrounging for something to eat. I had grand plans of eating away my worries when he told me you weren't feeling well. I decided to take advantage of your obviously fake illness and unburden my soul."

"What happened?" I asked suddenly concerned. "Why were you upset?"

She rolled her eyes. "My stupid ex is being a royal pain in my butt. He won't sign the divorce papers. He keeps dragging this out and making it more expensive. I don't understand why he's being so difficult."

"Maybe because he still wants you," Rosa said, softly.

"Well, he can't have me because he had everyone else," she shot back.

"I'm sorry," I said, meaning every word. The man deserved to be hexed. My earlier idea was looking better and better.

My mother came back inside. "I need to go," she said, her expression saying more than what her words were.

I nodded. "Okay."

She turned to Rosa. "Rosa, tell me what we should do with you."

I scoffed. "Like she's going to admit she'll betray us."

"I won't. I promise. I never wanted to hurt any of you. I reacted badly tonight and I am sorry, but I swear I will not reveal your secret," Rosa said, her eyes wide and earnest as she glanced among us.

"I believe you," my mother announced.

"Mom!" I shot back.

"Violet, trust me on this. I am confident we can count on Rosa to keep our secret safe."

Rosa was furiously nodding. "Yes, absolutely."

"Good. Do you need a ride home?" my mother asked.

"I can walk."

"No, let me drop you off," she insisted.

I realized then my mother wanted to scope out Rosa's house as well as keep her from running straight to Darlene, which she still could do in my opinion. Rosa stood with my mother's assistance. Daphne reluctantly returned her cane, giving her a stern look of warning before she released it.

"My mom texted," Daphne said, once my mother and Rosa were out the door. "We're supposed to take the chest to the factory."

I let out a long sigh. "I figured as much. Maybe we should wrap a blanket over the thing. It kind of freaks me out."

"We'll just make sure we don't jostle it and accidentally open the thing, if that's even possible."

"Let me change first and then we can go," I said, slowly standing, feeling every spot where the cane had connected with me.

It took me a little longer than usual to climb the stairs, but I managed. By the time we got to the factory, everyone else was already there. Daphne carried the chest in. I was too afraid I would trip and fall down the stairs. I envisioned the lid flying off and evil spinning into the air.

Daphne placed the chest on the small coffee table in the center of the seating area. Everyone stared at it, keeping their distance as if they were afraid it would bite. I was glad I wasn't the only one a little freaked out over the idea of a box of evil sitting in the room.

"You had an exciting night," Lila said with a smile on her face.

"Are you truly okay, dear?" Magnolia asked, looking me up and down.

"I'm fine. Bruised, but fine."

"We have to figure out a way to bust Darlene," Daphne said angrily.

"Yes, we do, and magic isn't the way to do it. I think we can assume she has that inkwell. Her position as an employee for the post office gives her access to all of our boxes," Coral chimed in.

I shook my head. I couldn't believe we hadn't figured that angle out earlier. It explained why the notes were always left in our post office boxes.

"Did she cast the calling out the witches spell?" I asked.

"Probably, but it was ineffective because her powers are bound. She likely put the note in your box to scare you," my mother answered.

"How are we going to make sure she pays for the crime?" Coral asked.

"Harold," Lila answered.

I couldn't hide my frustration at that suggestion. "Harold is useless as any kind of officer of the law."

"I'm going to undo the spell," she said matter-of-factly.

That grabbed Magnolia's attention. "You're what?"

"I found a spell that will undo my love spell."

"How! You know I tried for years," Magnolia said.

"I know hon, but I have been digging through old archives from other spell books. I'm convinced this will work. If it does, you can use it to undo your spell."

There were tears in Magnolia's eyes as she nodded.

"Okay, say the spell works and Harold is released from your love spell, how are we going to get him to go after Darlene?" I asked.

"We leave him clues. It won't take him long to figure it out. He was already leaning towards her as the culprit. We only need to gently push him in that direction," Lila explained.

I wasn't convinced, but I was willing to give it a shot. We couldn't exactly come right out and tell Harold why he should charge the woman with theft. In this situation, we had to let the man do his job. We couldn't use magic to hold the woman accountable, even if that was what I thought she deserved.

"Alright, assuming Harold takes care of Darlene, what are we to do about this Rosa woman?" Coral asked, always the one to keep the group on task.

"I wanted to check something," my mom said, walking out of sight and into a tiny room I had only seen once.

She returned holding what looked like a very old book. She put it on the table next to the chest. The lid on chest vibrated with her close proximity.

She looked at the chest and actually scolded it. "You hush. We'll take care of you in a minute."

I bit back a laugh. She was lecturing a wooden chest. Now, I had seen it all.

"What are you looking for, Mom?" I asked as her fingers ran over the pages of the book.

"There! I knew her name was familiar!"

"Whose name?" Lila asked. "I thought you guys already found Darlene's family name in the book."

"We did, but this is Rosa's family. The Herreras aren't from Lemon Bliss originally, but they did settle here for a short time before moving on. Their name is written in the book," she said, excitedly. "Rosa is a witch!"

"Does she know that?" I questioned.

"I don't think so, but it explains her natural tendency to protect the chest. She's a caretaker," my mother explained, a smile stretching across her face.

"How does she not know?" Daphne asked, her skepticism clear.

"The same way you didn't know," Magnolia reminded her.

"Wow," I mumbled. "Does that mean she's part of our coven?"

"No, it isn't quite so simple. We need to learn a little more about her and then of course, ask her. She may decide to deny that part of herself," my mother answered.

My mother stood and the chest rattled again. "Are we going to do something with that?" I asked, staring at the lid. "It seems dangerous to leave it sitting there. It's practically begging us to open it."

"Yes, it is. We'll need to find another chest to replace this one to keep anyone from asking questions," Coral said, seemingly enchanted by the vibrating box.

"Where?" Daphne blurted out. "That thing is ancient. I don't think there's another lying around."

"We'll get a forgery made. In the meantime, we keep this one here for safekeeping," Coral replied.

"Gabriel?" I offered his name. He had excellent carpenter skills.

Everyone looked at each other. For once, they agreed with me.

"I'll call him now," I said. "Let me take a couple of pictures to send to him so he can duplicate it."

I bent down close to the chest to take pictures of the ornate woodwork on the front. I was amazed at the power I could feel emanating from the wooden box. It was heady. I could understand the lure to open it and drink in that power.

Gabriel agreed to make the chest. He was half-asleep, but promised he would get up early to work on it. He even thought he could have it done by tomorrow night.

"So, we take the chest and give it to Harold?" I asked, wanting to make sure I had the plan clear in my mind.

"No, we have to let him find it in her possession," Coral clarified.

"But George already admitted he had it," I said, not intentionally trying to ruin their plan, but we had to think ahead.

"Harold didn't believe George. Lila convinced him to go pick it up, but once the spell is broken, he isn't going to be so inclined to do that. She has to charm him into doing it," Coral explained.

I nodded in understanding. "Okay, got it."

"Coral will go to Harold and tell him she saw Darlene carrying a strange chest. Then Lila will remember she heard Darlene talking to someone on the phone about how much the chest was worth. When he goes to question her, he is going to find it in the backseat of her car," my mother said, a smile on her face. "Oh to be a fly on the wall when she realizes she's busted!"

We all laughed at that. The plan wasn't full proof, but it was a start.

I looked at my watch and saw it was nearly one in the morning. "Are we good?"

"Yes. We'll take care of hiding this chest. It will never fall into the wrong hands again," Magnolia said. "We should have done this from the very beginning."

I agreed. I was glad to have half of our problems solved.

"Magnolia, do you want to stick around while I perform this spell?" Lila asked.

"Yes, please!"

Daphne and I waved goodbye and left them behind to take care of the details. Neither of us would be a lot of help. We didn't have the skills they did. It was better to leave something as important as hiding evil to the professionals in my book.

"I'll see you tomorrow," I told Daphne. "Bright and early."

"Don't remind me. Hopefully, you aren't too sore tomorrow."

"I better not be," I groaned, thinking of a long day standing on my sore leg.

By the time I got back home, locked up and crawled into bed, I was too tired to worry about Darlene or anything else.

CHAPTER 20

The next morning was a rough start for Daphne and me. I was dealing with a multitude of bruises and a sore foot. Not my best moment. Regardless of the heavy bags under our eyes and my aches and pains, we were both in high spirits. Today would hopefully be an end to weeks of stress and worry.

"Violet!" Daphne called out in a voice that sent shivers racing down my spine.

I dropped what I was doing and rushed up front to see what was wrong.

"What?"

"Harold's coming, and he doesn't look happy."

"Oh, crap," I mumbled.

He pulled open the door and took long strides to the front counter.

"Good morning, sheriff!" Daphne said with fake cheer in her voice. "Can I get you your usual? A chocolate chip cookie?"

His lip curled. I suddenly wondered if the love of the chocolate chip cookies was the result of Lila's love spell.

"Yes, that sounds good," he said in a gruff voice.

"I'll get it," I said, jumping for the case.

"Busy day?" Daphne pried.

He scowled. "Yep, got a hot lead that I hope will lead me to the culprit in that business over at the museum. Newcomers think they're going to come into my town and break laws. I don't think so."

I hid my smile as I reached into the case. Daphne rang him up, I put two cookies in a small bag, and he was gone.

We looked at each other, grinning like fools. "He's going to do it!" I declared.

"Hopefully, it all plays out. What if he goes over there and the chest isn't in place?"

"I'll call Gabriel right now," I said, trying not to panic.

Gabriel had gotten up early and went right to work on the chest. He planned on having it finished by mid-afternoon. I didn't want to rush him, but it was such a huge part of the plan.

"This better work," Daphne hissed as another customer came through the door.

I drifted back into the kitchen to get back to work. My mind was preoccupied, making it difficult to concentrate on baking. I burned several batches of cookies and dropped an entire pie on the floor.

"Violet!" Daphne called out from the front again.

I wiped my hands on my apron and walked out front to find my mother and Rosa taking a seat at one of the tables.

"What's that about?" I whispered.

Daphne shrugged. "Apparently, your mother has taken Rosa under her wing."

"Great," I muttered. While I appreciated my mother's kindness, I worried about how much Rosa knew. I supposed we'd have to hope for the best.

I walked over to their table and pulled up a chair to join them. Any excuse to get off my sore leg was welcome.

"What are you two up to?" I asked nonchalantly.

"I stopped by to see how Rosa was doing and discovered Darlene is threatening her," my mom announced.

"Threatened? How?"

"After you girls left last night, the others and I changed the plan. We felt it would be better coming from someone else."

"What came from someone else?"

"The tip. It's better to stick as close to the truth as possible. Rosa witnessed the theft. I spoke with her this morning. She went to Harold and told him everything. Harold questioned Darlene. It didn't take long for Darlene to figure out it was Rosa who turned her in."

"Ohh," I drew out, understanding the threats. "Why didn't Harold arrest her?"

"He's still investigating. We need to get that chest," she reminded me.

"I just talked with Gabriel. He said it would be done by this afternoon."

"Good. In the meantime, we need to keep Rosa close. I don't know how dangerous Darlene is, but we can't take any chances," my mother said.

Daphne stood by the table. "Is she actually threatening to hurt you?" she asked Rosa.

"Not hurt, but she knows I'm a witch," Rosa said.

Daphne and I exchanged a look. "You told her?" I asked my mother.

"Of course, I told her. She needs to know so she can be prepared."

"Oh. You seem to be taking it well," I said, looking to Rosa.

She smiled. "I have always suspected. I knew my mother believed herself to be a witch, but my father took me away from her when I was very little. I barely remembered her. When I was old enough, I tracked her down, but she had died years before. I had an aunt who gave me bits of information, which led me here to Lemon Bliss."

"She felt the calling," my mom said with a knowing smile.

"Welcome to Lemon Bliss," Daphne said. "I mean, I gather you've been here a while, but now you're one of us."

"We're taking things one step at a time," my mother said, a veiled message to keep the coven to ourselves.

"We should get back to work," I said, standing and limping back to the kitchen.

"I'll call if anything exciting happens," she said to my back.

I knew she would. I got back to work, doing my best to focus on the baking instead of magic and threats to reveal our deepest, darkest secret.

It was almost four in the afternoon and there had been no news of an arrest. I headed out front to double check with Daphne. Maybe she forgot to tell me. Of course, that would be crazy, but still.

"Any news?" I asked.

"Nope. Do you think Harold decided not to charge her?"

"I don't know. I'm going to call Gabriel and see if he delivered the chest to Coral. I feel like we've been left in the dark," I grumbled.

I called Gabriel and didn't get an answer. I was beginning to worry the plan had gone awry. Maybe Darlene had told Harold she believed we were all witches. What if he had arrested everyone else?

"I'm headed to my mom's the minute we close," I said.

"I've called my mom several times. Nothing. I'll go check on her while you check on your mom. Maybe Rosa was a plant."

My eyes widened at the idea. "Oh no. She may have told us all of that to get us to admit we were witches!"

Daphne was nodding her head. "She could have set up

Gabriel and the rest of them. If he got caught with the fake chest, Harold would believe Darlene!"

My heart raced. "We have to do something."

It was thirty minutes before closing. There had been no customers in the past thirty minutes.

"I'll make a sign," Daphne said, clearly reading my mind.

"I'll shut off the ovens."

I raced through the kitchen, putting everything away in record time. We were walking out the door five minutes later. Our plan was to divide and conquer. I drove straight to my mother's house only to find it empty.

"Is she there?" Daphne answered her phone.

"No! Is your mom home?"

"No!"

"Okay, I'll go by Gabriel's, you go by Coral's," I ordered before hanging up.

Gabriel's truck wasn't in the driveway I got out and knocked on the door anyway, just in case he was hiding out.

My phone rang. It was Daphne. "Anything?" I asked.

"No! What do we do? They just vanished!"

"Lila's?"

"I'm close, I'll check."

I sat in Gabriel's driveway, waiting for Daphne to call. I knew they wouldn't be there. Something was off. My phone rang again.

"Don't tell me, they're not there," I whispered.

"No."

Silence hung between us through the phone line. "The factory. Maybe they're hiding out at the factory."

"I'll meet you over there," Daphne said, disconnecting the call.

I drove too fast, but nearly screamed with relief and fury when I saw the myriad of cars in back. Gabriel's truck wasn't there, but at least we had found the rest of the women.

Daphne pulled in behind me. "Why aren't they answering their phones?" she said, angrily stomping towards the back door.

"I don't know, but we're going to find out."

We headed inside, and I could feel the magic in the air.

"What are they doing?" Daphne hissed as we walked downstairs.

I could hear the chanting and knew they were casting a spell. We paused at the foot of the stairs, waiting for them to be done. They were standing in a circle around the coffee table, their hands joined. I didn't know what kind of spell casting they were doing, but I didn't want to stop them midway.

After a few minutes, they dropped each other's hands and stepped back.

"Come in," my mother said, gesturing for us to enter the seating area.

"What were you doing?" I asked.

"Erasing Darlene's memories of us and all things witchy," Coral said calmly.

"Uh, was that a good idea?" I asked. "The inkwell is still out there and I'm guessing Darlene isn't under arrest."

"She should be getting the cuffs slapped on her right about now," Lila smiled.

Daphne flopped down in a chair. "You guys scared us to death! Why didn't you answer your phones?"

"We were a little busy, dear. Spells 101, you don't answer your phone when casting," Magnolia lectured.

"Where's Gabriel?" I asked, still worried.

"He took Rosa to drop off the chest. Rosa knows what Darlene drives. She's also apparently really good at picking a lock the non-magical way. Once they deliver the chest, Gabriel is supposed to take Rosa home and sit with her until we know Darlene is locked away. We had to wait to do the spell until it was the right time," my mother explained.

"You all need to work on your communication skills," I grouched.

"How do you know Darlene is getting arrested?" Daphne asked.

Lila winked. "We have our ways."

"And the spell?" I wondered aloud.

"We had to make sure she wouldn't follow through on her threats," Magnolia answered.

"So, it's over?"

"There is still the matter of the inkwell," my mom reminded me.

"I have a feeling it's in that post office. I'll go get it," I announced, happy to help bring it all to a nice, tidy end. "Is the real chest secured?"

"Yes. If you get the inkwell, we can erase its charm and return it to the museum for all to see," Coral said.

"Want to come along?" I asked Daphne.

She giggled. "Well, of course. I am your partner in crime. Breaking and entering is my thing now."

We left the factory and drove past Crooked Coffee and the post office. The sheriff's truck was nowhere in sight.

"I'll go in and get a coffee to make sure the post office is empty," Daphne said.

I stopped the car and let her out, driving around the block once more.

She jumped back in. "Coast is clear. Let's do this."

I drove around to the back and parked. It was a quick flick of my hand to unlock the door with my powers. We started to rifle through the backroom area.

"Found it!" Daphne shouted in a whisper, if that was possible.

She held up the inkwell with a grin on her face.

"I can't believe she had this the whole time," I mumbled.

"Let's get out of here. We'll take it back to the factory and let the moms do their voodoo magic to make it useless."

In short order, we returned to the factory with the inkwell in hand. Daphne and I waited while they removed any enchantments from the inkwell. The plan was to take it back to the post office and leave it in plain sight for someone to find. Everyone in town knew about the missing items from the museum. Hopefully, some alert citizen would turn it in and peace would be restored. If they didn't, it wasn't like the inkwell was a threat. I didn't care. It could sit on someone's desk if they wanted it.

I was all too happy to have it all behind us. Life would return to normal once again. I could enjoy the success of the bakery and my growing relationship with Gabriel. I was also looking forward to getting my witch practice back on track. I felt inept, and I didn't like that feeling at all. I wanted to be strong and powerful and confident in myself and my gifts.

EPILOGUE

George Cannon was angry and a little hurt. He had been questioned repeatedly about the theft that happened at the museum, and he was sick of it. It wasn't his fault the sheriff hadn't bothered to get off his butt and pick up the chest from his back porch. It didn't matter how many times he said it, no one seemed to believe he was innocent.

Instead of sticking around and waiting for the sheriff to show up and wrongly arrest him, he had holed up in New Orleans the last few days, securing supplies to run a real supernatural investigation. He had avoided Lemon Bliss until it was safe to go back and the threat of being hauled off to jail was gone.

When Darlene Clayton had finally been arrested and charged with the theft, he had expected an apology. It never happened. The people in Lemon Bliss thought he was an idiot. He was going to prove them wrong while working on his big break into the supernatural world of investigations. He was a solo act now. He would get all the glory, like he deserved.

He was on a mission to prove his late friend had been on to something, while elevating his own status in the world of supernatural investigations.

George parked his car in front of the sheriff's building and smoothed his shirt before slicking back his hair. He took a look in the rearview mirror and decided he looked the part he was about to play.

"Hello, I called earlier about visiting a person you're holding," George said to the elderly woman sitting at the desk.

"We don't allow visitors," she replied.

"I already arranged it with the sheriff," George said smoothly.

The elderly woman looked at her desk as if the answer was there. "Well he didn't tell me anything. Who are you wanting to see?"

"Darlene Clayton," George replied. "I'm her lawyer," he lied.

"She's scheduled to be transported to the county jail later today."

George nodded as if he already knew about the transfer. He didn't, but he was glad he came when he did. He had purposely waited out front until he saw the sheriff leave.

Darlene was sitting in one of the two cells in the small building.

"Hello, Darlene," George said in an authoritative voice.

She looked at him as if she didn't recognize him.

"I'm George Cannon, your attorney," he said in a low voice.

She cocked her head to the side before nodding slowly.

"Can I have a minute alone with my client?" he asked, turning to the receptionist who was hanging on their every word.

"Fine."

Once the receptionist left the area, George eyed Darlene. "What happened to you?

"What do you mean?"

"You seem different."

She shrugged a shoulder. "I'm in jail. I am different."

"Do you have that book you told me about or that inkwell?" he asked her.

"What book? What inkwell?" she echoed, confusion on her face.

"You told me you had a magical inkwell that was charmed in some way. You also said you had a book that could prove my theory about Lemon Bliss," he reminded her.

She shook her head. "I don't know what you're talking about. Prove what about Lemon Bliss?"

George stared at the young woman. He couldn't tell if she was faking her sudden amnesia, or if something had truly caused her to forget what she had told him.

He cleared his throat, a little nervous to say his next words. "You told me you knew there were witches living in Lemon Bliss."

She grinned. "You're nuts. Maybe you should be locked up in here instead of me."

"You gave me that chest! You said it held some kind of power!"

She cocked her head to the side. His hopes were raised. It looked like she was remembering something. "I don't know what you're talking about."

George threw his hands in the air and growled. "I knew I couldn't trust you!"

He stomped out of the jail, furious with the woman who had led him on a wild goose chase. He wasn't going to give up. An idea sprang to mind. He turned around and headed back down the street to the new little bakery in town. He didn't have concrete evidence, but he could put pressure on the woman he knew had knowledge of what was going on in Lemon Bliss.

"Hi," the young bubbly woman behind the counter greeted him as he walked through the door.

"Good morning," he responded.

This bakery was a hub of activity, which meant people would be chatting and gossiping without realizing he was listening to their every word. His plan was to charm and disarm—starting now.

"What can I get for you?" the woman who wore a nametag identifying her as Daphne said, a little perkier than he cared for.

"I'd like a blueberry muffin and a coffee please."

The woman eyed him a little too closely. He saw the instant she realized who he was.

Her cheery demeanor changed. With barely a smile, there was a muffin shoved into his hand and a cup of coffee slammed onto the counter.

He smiled. She didn't like him. Few people did.

"Is that it?" she asked, her tone frosty.

"Yes, thank you. I think I'll sit right over there and enjoy my breakfast."

Daphne simply nodded and turned to greet the next customer. Her business partner here at the bakery owned the factory was his friend was killed. She had accused him of stealing the chest and had the audacity to actually come to his house and say it to his face. He didn't like her and if his presence in her bakery irritated her, then his mission would be successful. He intended to hound her until she broke.

As he sat enjoying what he hated to admit was a really good muffin, the only person that had shown him any kindness walked through the door.

"George," Gabriel said when he spotted him in the corner.

"Gabriel, join me for a quick breakfast," he invited.

Gabriel looked to the counter and then back to George.

"Sure, let me get something and I'll be right over," he replied.

George watched as the girl at the counter and Gabriel exchanged a few words in hushed tones. He had a feeling they were talking about him. Let them talk, he thought. In his mind, everyone living in the town of Lemon Bliss was hiding the truth.

When Gabriel sat across from him at the table, he was friendly enough, but George was still suspicious. It was in his nature to question everything and everybody.

"I hear that whole museum business has finally come to an end," George said, trying to get the other man talking.

"I heard the same thing. It's unfortunate the woman tried to frame you. Did you know her?"

"No, no. I met her a few times at the post office, but our dealings never went beyond that," George lied.

They had actually had many meetings. Darlene provided him with plenty of information about the people in Lemon Bliss. She wouldn't give him names. She had promised to reveal more if he allowed her to be a part of the special he was putting together. She was in it for revenge and he wanted fame. They had made a good team.

Until she had screwed up and gotten herself arrested.

"Well, it sounds like she had a history of doing that kind of thing. I'm glad the sheriff was able to track her down and lock her up. We don't need that here in Lemon Bliss," Gabriel said.

"I came here to Lemon Bliss to complete my investigation, but I sure have grown fond of the place and the people," George said, using his most charming tone.

Gabriel eyed him closely, making George squirm a little.

"I hope you understand the people around here like to live quiet lives. With this new special you're planning to air,

I hope you'll keep all that in mind. We like our privacy around here."

George finished his coffee and leaned on his elbows on the table. "I said I like Lemon Bliss, but I like to uncover the truth more. If the good people that live here in Lemon Bliss have a story that needs telling, I intend to tell it, with or without the approval of the town."

Gabriel shook his head slowly. "That's really too bad, George. I had hoped we could be friends."

George stood and shrugged one shoulder. "I don't really need friends. I need the respect and recognition that goes along with being a renowned supernatural investigator. Believe it or not, your little town and your friends are going to be what brings me what I want."

As George headed for the door, he could feel eyes on him. He turned to see Violet Broussard standing beside her friend behind the counter. He glared back at them. They had a secret, and he was going to uncover it.

George headed back to the old farmhouse he was renting and pulled out his notebook. Darlene had given him plenty of information. He had been working diligently to follow up on everything. The woman was a little off her rocker, but she had been onto something. The items she pilfered from the museum had history, and it had nothing to do with their age.

He knew there was something special about that chest. He had felt it. When he tried to pry it open, his suspicions had been confirmed.

He slammed the notebook shut, tucked it into his back pocket, grabbed his phone and headed out the door. It was time to do some real investigating.

George drove around the massive factory, making sure it was empty. That Violet thought she was so smart by locking up that side door. He knew another way in. After looking left and then right, he knocked over the large wooden spool that had been pushed against a wall. He climbed on top and pushed open the old-fashioned window.

It was how he and Dale had gained entry until they managed to break the lock on the side door. Once inside the factory, he dusted off and took a look around. The first thing he did was head up to the fourth floor. They had left equipment in one of the offices. He was hoping it was still there. It was time to start surveillance on the place again, but this time, he was going to be far more careful. The women would never know he was watching.

George explored the fourth floor, using the camera on his phone to take pictures before moving down to the third floor. By the time he reached the ground floor, he already knew where he would place the cameras.

He walked the ground floor, searching for something. He didn't know what, but he knew there was something here that drew Dale in. Dale was always better at that kind of thing. He had instinct, something George knew he was lacking.

It didn't matter. He'd find out by using technology and snooping. Whatever got the job done. He was a little disappointed he didn't find anything, but he wasn't going to give up. There was something here. He would find it.

IF YOU'D LIKE updates when I have new releases and other news, sign up for my newsletter: https://lucymayauthor.com/subscribe

FOR MORE FUN with the witches in Lemon Bliss, turn the page for a sneak peek from Witch is When it Gets Crazy, the next book in the Lemon Tea Series.

EXCERPT: WITCH IS WHEN IT GETS CRAZY

CHAPTER 1

*T*he buzz of voices from beyond the kitchen door filtered into the bakery kitchen. Business was humming along, and I was thrilled. Lemon Bliss wasn't exactly a booming town, yet I'd wanted to take the chance because I needed a viable way to remain in Lemon Bliss and my bestie Daphne was a major cheerleader for the idea. Not to mention, she was my business partner. Lemon Bliss was just large enough to have enough people to keep us busy. It also helped that we happened to be the only bakery in town.

"Violet?" Patty, my newest staff member, called my name from the front.

Daphne was off today, something we agreed we both deserved. We were coming up on six months of the bakery both being open *and* running in the black. It was time to hire staff and enjoy the fruits of our labor. Since Daphne was off today, that meant I was on. Honestly, I was always on, even if I said I was taking the day off.

"Coming," I called out, quickly pulling the cookies from the oven before hurrying to the front. Patty was new and tended to panic if she saw more than a few people in line.

Walking out front, I saw the dining area was filled and there were several people in line at the register. I was surprised Patty had waited so long to call me for help. As I scanned the customers, my eyes landed on my mother. She didn't look happy with her lips tightened to a line and her arms crossed as she tapped her foot.

I inwardly groaned, hoping there wasn't yet another disaster that needed my immediate attention. Since I'd been back in Lemon Bliss, it felt as if there had been one crisis after another. It had been peaceful the past couple of months, and I had hoped I was on the way to a more peaceful life.

One look at my mother and my senses started tingling, announcing the idea of peace was about to blow up in my face. I just knew it. When she saw me come through the swinging door out front, she started to approach the counter.

"Just a second, Mom," I called, turning my attention to the line.

After we took care of everyone in line, I gestured for my mom to follow me into the kitchen. I didn't need the entire bakery to hear about our latest problem.

"Patty, holler if you need me," I told her, making sure the kitchen door closed behind us. My mother started pacing back and forth in front of my worktable, twisting her hands as she did. Her charm bracelets clinked softly with the movement.

"Oh, Violet. We've got a problem," she said as she paced her way past me.

"What now, Mom? Something missing? Someone died? What? What could be so wrong?" I asked, beating back my frustration. I *really* wanted a normal life. Although ever since I'd learned I was a witch, normal seemed hard to come by.

She stopped pacing, pinning her gaze to me. "Someone did die, Violet, and it is not funny in the slightest."

Panic and worry hit me. "Who?!" I exclaimed, my heart racing.

"We didn't know him all that well, but I knew *of* him. The fact he was so young is what's terrible. That and the reality that his death spells more trouble for all of us."

"Who?" I asked, frustration making my voice shrill. "Who died?"

"Harry."

"Who?" I asked, blinking and quickly trying to place a face with the name.

"Harry. He was working with that awful man, George," my mother said, her mouth twisting.

My mother was *not* fond of George, but then neither was I. George was the supernatural investigator who'd been out to get us for months now. He just would not give up on the idea he could unmask the supernatural secrets in Lemon Bliss. Since we were witches who very much wanted to keep our existence a secret, we kept bumping up against his aggressive curiosity.

"How did Harry die?" I asked the next obvious question. I still hadn't sorted out why my mother was worried beyond the general concern when someone dies.

"Violet, you don't understand. Harry was one of the supernatural investigators. Rumors are flying around town that Harry died after visiting the factory last night."

I bit back a curse. "What?! Why was he in the factory? Why do they keep going there? Why can't they just stay out? It's private property and mine. No one has permission to be there. Did he die there?"

A suspicious death in the abandoned lemon tea factory my grandmother had bequeathed to me was what had originally brought me back to Lemon Bliss. Sweet tea! If someone else died there, it would be even harder to keep suspicions off the witches.

"I have no idea if Harry was actually there, but that's what people are saying. As far as I can sort out, he was found dead at his home this morning, so he must not have died at the factory. I thought you should know right away. It's just terrible."

Leaning my hips against the table running through the center of the kitchen, I sighed. "Wow. I can't believe this. Another supernatural investigator turning up dead is just downright weird."

My mother leaned against the table beside me. "I know. Even though the first death was an accident, it just drew attention to the old factory. And George! My word, that man just won't let it go. Apparently, he brought in a couple of friends who are also supernatural investigators. And of course, the factory is the center of his investigation. I'm guessing that's why Harry was at the factory last night. They must be sneaking in again."

"Mom, when did you hear George was looking into the factory again?" I asked, glancing to her.

She took a deep breath. "George brought in Dale's son to continue his father's work."

"Dale?"

"The man that died in the factory almost six months ago," she said as if I were an idiot.

"Oh, right. Sorry, I wasn't thinking."

"Anyway, Dale Junior brought along his college buddy Harry, and Stan. Apparently, Stan worked with Dale Senior in the past. The men have been working on that stupid investigation. The ladies and I have been keeping an eye on things as much as we can without being obvious," she explained. "I didn't want to mention it to you because I didn't want you to worry. We figured eventually they'd get bored and move on. Now someone else turns up dead. What a mess."

I sighed and rolled my head from side to side, trying to ease the tension building in my neck.

"Anyway, the police called me this morning," she added.

"Why did they call you?"

"Because they couldn't get a hold of you."

"Okay, why were they trying to call me?"

She released a long, heavy sigh. "Because George told them about being at the factory and said he thinks something happened to Harry there. Of course, the police don't care those men have been breaking and entering and trespassing at will. But they're happy to assume something nefarious happened even though Harry didn't actually die at the factory," she said, her tone snippy.

"I can't be responsible for every single thing that happens around here, and neither can you. This is really getting old!"

"I'm sorry, dear. I know this is not what you expected when you moved back home."

"I have a feeling this is going to be the new normal. If only I could get those supernatural investigators to stop sneaking into the factory. I don't care about their silly investigations, but for crying out loud, they shouldn't be breaking in! Every two or three months, someone is going to do something that threatens our coven. Mom, are you sure this whole witch thing is really worth all this trouble?" I asked softly.

"Yes. We can't change who we are even if we wanted to. We have to protect our secret, which is what we've all been doing for decades, and what we will keep doing. Now, right now, you need to go talk with the sheriff. I don't know if it will be Harold asking the questions, or someone else."

"I'm working, Mom. I can't up and leave Patty by herself."

"I could stay," she offered.

I bit back my laugh. I wasn't sure if that was her intention, but the idea was laughable. "I'll call, Daphne," I said with resignation.

"I'm sorry to drop this on you, Violet. I promise, recent events are not the norm. It's this George character. Once we can figure out how to get rid of him, our troubles will be over," she said.

As if it was that simple. I seriously doubted it.

Pushing away from the counter, I walked to the back to grab my purse and phone. When I turned to look at her, my spidey-sense started tingling again. "Mom, what are you planning?" I asked.

She shrugged. "Oh, good grief! You always assume the worst. I'm just thinking."

At that, she walked out of the kitchen. Standing there, I took a deep breath. Things were getting weird. Well, they'd already been more than weird. Could it really be a coincidence these two men died after visiting the factory? The factory built on the location of the site of coven meetings for a few centuries. I'd had my suspicions before, but I'd tried mightily to ignore them.

"No way, Violet. This is no coincidence," I murmured into the empty kitchen.

I had to start facing reality. Something wasn't quite right in Lemon Bliss, and I was beginning to wonder if it ever would be. It certainly didn't feel like it.

Fishing my cell phone out of my purse, I called Daphne. So much for her day off. I hated to disturb her, but I had to talk with Harold right away. Daphne understood my predicament and promised to be right in.

Within minutes, she breezed into the kitchen through the back door. "Hey, tell me everything. Do I need to pack my bags? Are we running?" she asked by way of greeting.

I rolled my eyes. "No, unless you want to tell me something," I said, raising an eyebrow.

She scoffed. "I'm not even sure what I supposedly did. So, what happened? Another dead guy in the factory? I can't even believe that."

I shook my head. "Actually, not in the factory, but his buddies told the police he was in the factory and then dropped dead shortly afterwards."

She released a long sigh. "And the police want to talk to you to find out if you somehow magically killed this guy all because he trespassed in the factory?"

I nodded. "Sounds about right."

"Do you ever regret moving back?" she said, softly.

I took a few seconds to think it over. "No. I regret that two people have died, but I have a feeling those deaths would have happened whether I was here or not."

"Technically, you weren't here for the first."

"True, but I do feel bad the man died, especially on my property. Another regret I have is not securing that factory better. You would think they would learn their lesson, though. I mean, if they really think the factory is haunted, and bad things seem to happen when they go there, why do they keep going back?" I asked.

Daphne laughed. "So true. On the one hand, they keep insisting the factory is going to give them the supernatural scoop of the century, and on the other, they keep putting themselves in danger in a place they claim is dangerous." She paused, her gaze sobering. "Honestly though, if he didn't die there, I'm sure it will be resolved. It had nothing to do with you, so they'll figure it out."

"Let's hope so. Anyway, I better get down there. I'm so sorry I had to bring you in on your day off. I'll work for you on my day off."

"Don't worry about it, Violet. I wasn't actually doing anything anyway. I hope you did a lot of baking already though. You know I'm not so good back here," she said with a rueful smile.

Baking wasn't Daphne's contribution to the business. "Everything's done. You should have plenty of stock to get through the rest of the day. If not, just say we're sold out," I said with a weak smile.

"Or they could just leave," she quipped.

"We'll worry about that later. For now, let's make sure we don't go to jail."

Her eyes narrowed as she sobered again, stepping close to me. "Do you think it was one of them?"

I knew exactly who she was talking about because I'd had the very same thought. I hated myself for it, but it seemed like there was always one common denominator— my mother and her friends, one of whom was Daphne's mother. The members of our coven were somehow at the center of yet another crime.

"I don't know, Daphne. I don't want to believe they could have had anything to do with this, but we know how protective they are of that factory."

"Okay, so we get this latest crisis taken care of, and then what? Are we going to constantly be forced to put out these little fires when we least expect it? Why do we have to use that stupid factory anyway? You have insurance on it, right?"

I didn't like where she was going with that question. "Of course I do."

"Then let's burn it to the ground," she said, matter-of-factly.

I laughed, then quickly stopped when I realized she wasn't joking. "No! Daphne, don't even think like that. If that factory burns, I'm coming to you," I warned.

She shrugged, "Just saying, it seems to be the root of all of our problems."

"You can't blame a building for what people do."

"Fine. Go do what you need to. I'll hold down the fort. Be careful, Violet. I have a feeling you're going to be a suspect, again."

"I know, and I will. I'll call you if I find out anything. Thanks, Daphne."

With a wave, I quickly grabbed my purse and left.

COPYRIGHT © *2018 LUCY MAY; All rights reserved.*

* * *

AVAILABLE NOW!

Witch is When it Gets Crazy

Be sure to sign up for my newsletter. I promise - no spam! Click here to sign up: https://lucymayauthor.com/subscribe

MY BOOKS

Thank you for reading A Spell to Tell! I hope you enjoyed the magic. If so, here are a few ways to help other readers find my books.

1) Write a review!
2) Sign up for my newsletter, so you can receive information on new releases:
https://lucymayauthor.com/subscribe
3) Like my Facebook page at
https://www.facebook.com/lucymayauthor/

* * *

Lemon Tea Cozy Mysteries
Witch You Wouldn't Believe
A Spell to Tell
Witch is When it Gets Crazy

Wicked Good Mystery Series

Destiny's A Witch - coming August 2018
Hex Me Not - coming October 2018
Spells & Silver Bells - coming December 2018

ACKNOWLEDGMENTS

Many thanks to my readers for reminding me magic is possible—in more ways than one.

Cosmic Letterz did a fabulous job designing the covers for this series. This story was inspired by a few funny life events, including the shared joy of exploring old places with my husband. Thanks to him for making every journey fun.

No story would be complete without the interruptions of my dogs who know how to lift my spirits on any day.

xoxo

Lucy May

ABOUT THE AUTHOR

Lucy May loves coffee, dogs, cooking, and writing. She's a misplaced Southerner living in Maine. She's grown to love four seasons, but she still pines for sleepy southern summers. She likes to think she might've been a witch in another life and still believes in magic. She wiles away her time spinning snarky, witchy & sexy paranormal stories.

f

CPSIA information can be obtained
at www.ICGtesting.com
Printed in the USA
BVHW042220260520
580380BV00010B/313